# RIDING ON
# HORSES'
# WINGS

# RIDING ON HORSES' WINGS

*Reimagining Today's Horse
for Tomorrow's World*

## JANET BUBAR RICH

Kravitz & Sons

INNOVATORS IN PUBLISHING, MARKETING AND ADVERTISING

**Kravitz and Sons LLC**
1301 Farmville Blvd, Suite 104
Greenville, NC 27834



Published by Kravitz and Sons LLC.

ISBN:        979-8-89639-309-2   (sc)
ISBN:        979-8-89639-308-5   (e)
ISBN:        979-8-89639-314-6   (hb)

Library of Congress Control Number: 2025909496

# Dedication

To my family and friends, for helping me find my wings.
To all horses, mythological and otherwise,
who inspire us to ride on our souls' journeys.
And to Pegasus, who inspires many of us to reach for the Stars.

# TABLE OF CONTENTS

# Preface

When I bestride him, I soar, I am a hawk:
he trots the air; the earth sings when he touches it.
  –William Shakespeare (*Henry V*, Act III)[1]

Sitting amidst a herd of cars in the hot afternoon on our way into West L.A., I scratched my head in wonder: How did we get here? I know we arrived at this location by driving a short distance from our neighborhood. I mean: How did our civilization get to this point in which we each buy a car, gas or charge it up, and drive (often one person per vehicle) straight into a traffic jam?

Suddenly it occurred to me: It all started with a horse and a human's passion to ride. The distance from that moment in history to this did not take long. It simply required humankind's imaginative technological advancements. Although traffic jams in urban environments across the world are getting worse, increasing the time consumed in getting to our destinations, we each continue to mount our high-horsepower vehicles with the same passion our forebears honored and rode their horses.

The human and horse (now car, with its engine's performance measured in "horsepower") relationship is deep. For humans, horses provide freedom. Horses (now high-horsepower cars) are our wings. They empower us to ride on journey's going farther and faster than we can on our own. As a result, their image shows up in our dreams, waking lives, and, hence, our personal and cultural stories, as symbols not only of freedom, but of power, swiftness, and beauty, empowering us to ride on inner journeys, explore the mysteries of the soul, and carry the human spirit forward. In delving into the horse tales of many cultures throughout the ages and weaving them together into this book, inspired by my hopping into high-horsepower cars and sitting in the traffic jams that yield time to ponder, my hope is to shed light on the depth of humankind's fascination with horses—now *"horsepower"*.

**Notes**

[1]William Shakespeare, *The Life of Henry V*, ed. John Russell Brown (NY and Ontario: Signet Classic, New American Library, 1965), 103.

# CHAPTER 1

# Introduction

*Riding on Horses' Wings: Reimagining Today's Horse for Tomorrow's World* speaks of humans' deep-seated love of horses and the horse tales that have permeated our diverse cultures across the globe for centuries. It speaks of humans' enduring love of swift powerful horses as expressed in myths and dreams, a love that, in our technological age, has become the love of cars with high *horsepower*, a term coined by James Watt in the eighteenth century for a unit used to measure the power of engines. With concerns about the effects of human activity on the earth and its inhabitants, this book puts forth a call to channel the love of horses to a concern for horses' survival, the love of riding to an effort to reduce driving, and an obsession with horsepower to the power of humans to make changes needed for the survival of horses and other species on earth, our home. Finally, it looks at wondrous horse tales that speak to the human soul in cadences only tales of horses can.

Galloping through myths, fairytales, and dreams, horses inspire those who behold them and lift the hearts of those who befriend them. From the white-winged steed Pegasus in ancient Greek mythology, Epona in Celtic mythology, and the Kelpies in Scottish folklore, to Sleipner in Norse mythology and Kanthaka in Buddhist mythology, magical stallions from diverse cultures have been romping around the human psyche for eons. Now in the literary, performing, and visual arts, and in movies, TV shows, YouTubes, podcasts, videogames, product logos, and beyond, horses are being broadcast and revered as heroes, with products and companies bearing their names.

Horses are prevalent in pop culture. Such TV-show notables as Silver in *The Lone Ranger* (1933), Trigger in *Roy Rogers* (1950s), and the talking horse in *Mister Ed* (1960s) feed our fantasies of loyalty, friendship, and bravery. *Seabiscuit* (2003), *Secretariat* (2010), and *War Horse* (2011) are among the myriad movies about horses that have thrilled audiences worldwide. Also, a mega-million-dollar horse race industry attracts exuberant crowds who bet their dreams on horses such as California Chrome and American Pharoah, capturing fans' heartbeats with every hoof beat.

Horse tales, like romances, lift the human spirit with a vitality that vivifies and awakens imaginations from deeper spheres. Capturing the hearts of those who want to believe in something beyond themselves, mythmakers from diverse cultures throughout the centuries have been spinning horse tales, myths, and lore forward, as this book reveals. Triumphs of Pegasus, Seabiscuit, Secretariat, and so many other horse heroes come to life in vivid grit. Against all odds, these horses overcome disadvantages and hardships to achieve their destinies and their owners' dreams. Touching human hearts and healing human spirits, their breathtaking tales offer examples of personal and universal transformations that invigorate audiences to face challenges in their lives with the confidence to realize their dreams.

*Riding on Horses' Wings: Reimagining Today's Horse for Tomorrow's World* looks at horses in the myths of diverse cultures, offering brief reflections to reimagine the myths for today. This book culminates with a discussion about the depth of the human and horse bond. For, while the adoration of horses easily becomes an adoration of high-horsepower cars especially among today's urban dwellers who depend on their shiny computerized steeds to take them where they want to go, opportunities emerge to reflect on ways in which humans can slide their devotion to and dependence on these cars into the support of horse (and human) survival on earth. By stilling our minds to listen and hear the horses, then consciously taking our lives by the reins, we may be able to create sustainable futures for ourselves and other earth residents.

In addition, this book is written with the hope of inspiring those who seek to make personal life changes. These changes might include re-skilling to launch or revitalize careers, starting families, adjusting to children leaving or aging parents returning to their homes, or, navigating personal aging or health issues. Worse, the changes might be responding to natural disasters that require moving to new locations or rebuilding lives and livelihoods. Such changes involve redefining oneself. Everyone needs to make or respond to changes when they are at crossroads—having heroes and role models who have survived such changes may help provide pathways.

In these horse tales from varied cultures that come to life, readers may see through adventures and themes to truths. Myths such as these about wild, tame, and gallant horses erupt from and inform our imaginations. As symbols, personifications, and images, they provide role models and roadmaps that influence the choices we make that shape our lives.

Unlike other animals, humans are storytellers. The stories we create in turn create us. Their characters influence our ideas about who we are and might become. For psychoanalyst Carl Gustav Jung, to be conscious means to be aware of and engage with archetypes. Looking at horse myths as archetypal, therefore, allows us to see the archetypes that are active within ourselves and our communities.

Why explore horse archetypes and themes? Among the many motivations is that mythic characters and stories mirror our past and possibilities. Looking at them may help us reimagine blueprints for our own lives moving forward. Seeing how the horses transform their lives and those of their riders elevates our sense of being able to overcome obstacles, take life by the reins, meet challenges, and create sustainable futures.

# Book's Roadmap

*Chapter 1: Introduction* provides an overview of the author's intention in writing the book as well as this roadmap for the journey ahead.

*Chapter 2: Mythological Horses* provides a mythological and psychological framework for exploring horse tales as archetypes at work within us and our world and offers insights into horses' symbolic meaning.

*Chapter 3: Horses in Ancient Greek and Celtic Mythologies* presents the transformative tales of Pegasus, the Trojan horse, centaurs, and other horses from ancient Greek mythologies, … and the mythical white horses, protector of horses, and more from the ancient Celtic lore.

*Chapter 4: Horses of Norse Mythology* discusses the meaning of many wondrous mythological horses in Norse mythology, including the magical eight-legged warhorse Sleipner, son of Loki by the stallion Svaoilfari. It offers insights into Sleipner's being gifted to Odin, God of noblemen and kings while Thor, God of the common man, does not ride a horse.

*Chapter 5: Mythological Horse Tales from Asia* looks at the horse in Hindu and Buddhist mythologies. This chapter presents a variety of horse tales from India, Japan, Tibet, China, Korea, the Philippines, and Vietnam, and offers a Caspian horse tale from Persia, now Iran.

*Chapter 6: Horse Mythologies in Monotheistic Cultures* explores the horses' role in legends from Arab, Jewish, and Christian traditions and lore, as well as some mystery and magic surrounding the unicorn.

*Chapter 7: Native American Horse Tales* presents the deep relationships of Native Americans with horses and the tales that emerge as a result. Affection, friendship, and the deep bonds between people and their horses come into focus.

*Chapter 8: Saddling Up with Horse Tales* probes horse imagery in literature, poetry, and the visual arts, and speaks of humans' love of horses and horse tales. Exploring horse imagery in many art forms allows us to appreciate the vibrancy of the human and horse relationship.

*Chapter 9: Contemporary Horse Tales* shed light on how contemporary myth- or filmmakers reimagine horse tales reflecting the yearnings and inspirations of individuals and cultures, and how songwriters carry hoof beats into our sound waves. Finally, it speaks of humans' enduring love of swift powerful horses as expressed in myths and dreams that come to life on the silver screen, YouTubes, and the latest media.

*Chapter 10: Horsepower vs Horse Survival* suggests people today hop into their dream cars and ride off into the sunset just as their forebears had hopped onto their horses. Car companies know that connecting their products with our passions bring them big bucks, and many hop on board. With concerns about the earth's changing climate and depleting natural resources, this chapter presents the value of securing horses' and other species' survival.

# CHAPTER 2

## Mythological Horses

Running free with their manes and tails flying, horses inspire the mythic imagination. Dashing across fields and prairies as well as through myths, fairytales, and dreams, the spirited creatures galvanize those who behold them and lift the hearts of those who befriend them. Responding to danger, reacting to changes in the terrain, and instinctively defending themselves and their foals, the steeds heighten our awareness of our surroundings and alert us to the characteristics needed to survive.

Being with horses offers humans authentic experiences of being alive. Accordingly, horse images evoke these authentic experiences and connect humans with the rhythms of the natural world and the drive toward spiritual ascent. As live horses as well as today's high-horsepower vehicles carry people farther and faster than they can walk, symbolic horses empower people to ride on inner journeys, traverse passages and pathways, and charge forth into spiritual skies to explore the mysteries of the soul and carry the human spirit forward.

Exploring horse tales from a wide range of traditions allows us to appreciate the depth of history and bond humans and horses share. Delving into horse myths across many cultures reveals humankind's fascination with horses. Finally, looking at horse archetypes and their significance and meaning in many mythologies reveals how, as a universal symbol of the imagination, the horse can help us understand our own place and meaning in today's world.

# Myths Nourish Imaginations

When we mythologize, we engage the imagination to help us carve meaning out of life-changing events and circumstances. With understanding comes acceptance or the motivation to make changes. Personal myths allow us to see ourselves; cultural myths allow us to see the society in which we live. Stories are built around our personal and universal needs; telling stories connects us. While we create stories, they create us.[1] Though mythologies may differ from culture to culture, we often see through them to universal patterns and truths.

People need and spawn stories, dream in stories; cultures need and produce myths. When breaking out of old paradigms and seeking new ones, people yearn for guiding stories. Upon reflection, it is illuminating to see the archetypes with which we identify, for these tell us something about our own personal mythologies around which we construct our identities and lives. According to C. G. Jung, people need to understand the myths in which they are living in order to understand the new myths into which they might move.

# Emergence: New Self Concept

Horses throughout the mythologies of many lands are symbols of transformation and transcendence. Such symbols pull at those who are situated at life's crossroads and ready to make the choices that will change their lives. Tales from across the globe of magical steeds overcoming challenges not only to survive but to accomplish great deeds offer us inspiration. Tales of horse riders attending to, teaming up with, and trusting horses; living in the moment; taking chances; using instincts, intuition, and powers of focus and concentration; and letting go to enjoy the ride— inspire us to take life by the reins.

Many people love horses. Looking at horse archetypes to see those with which we identify may help us get to know ourselves and find new pathways. Viewing archetypes from the perspective of C. G. Jung helps root this discussion about horse archetypes within the mythic and psychoanalytic traditions that seek to find life's meaning and purpose by probing the unconscious. Adding a historical perspective helps provide a broad understanding of horse iconography and imagery, and their meaning for us today.

# Archetypes: C. G. Jung

Everyone's brain produces similar patterns regardless of life experiences, observes Jung. These major patterns of experiencing the world, Jung calls *archetypes*. Archetypes in Jung's psychology are defined as factors and motifs that arrange psychic elements into certain images, characterized as archetypal, but in such a way that they can be recognized only from the effects they produce. Expressed another way, they are the array of psychological patterns or innate ideas that human beings possess for interpreting events and observations.

Expressing themselves in actions that are similar in each of us, archetypes seem to be instinctive. They show up as symbols. People encounter them as they listen to stories, read books, and watch movies. They recognize them in their own emotional tugs as they watch mythical characters handling the emotional pleasures and pains associated with the changes, conflicts, gains, and losses with which they wrestle in their own lives.

# Introducing Horse Archetypes

Widely regarded for centuries as magnificent, powerful, and magical beings, the horses humans have encountered have inspired some fantastic creatures to spring from the human imagination and touch human hearts. The horse, according to Jung, is a common vision that emerges in the activity of the collective unconscious, and the horse archetype has multiple meanings. As an animal, it represents the non-human psyche, or the person's animal side, the *unconscious*. For Jung,

"Legend attributes properties to the horse which psychologically belong to the unconscious of [humans]." For example, path-finding horses lead lost wanderers to their destinations.[2] As Jung avows, "The horse . . . plays the part of the psychopump [or mediator] who leads the way to the other world,"[3] with *other world* to mean the unconscious. Here, the horse is the archetypal image of hope and help, as he accompanies humans through isolation and chaos.

Further, Jung discusses a vision told to him of a buckskin-clad Aztec boy named Chiwantopel who arrives on horseback. In this vision, Chiwantopel refers to his horse as "his faithful brother" (Jung, *Symbols* 274), revealing that the horse and rider have an intimate connection. While searching for a soul mate, the Aztec is attacked by a snake (symbolic of death and destruction, or fertility, birth, and rebirth) that bites him and kills his horse (symbolic of transcending or becoming). The conflict of the heart this represents is common as adults who, in moving toward a new identity or status quo, first must kill their old identity, or security. The hero must free himself from *what is* in order to ride the horse forward, or gallop toward that which he might *become*. In this vision, the hero is stultified, as their intimate connection leads them to a shared destiny.

Looking across cultures, Jung finds the same archetypes operating and thus comes to conceptualize them as fundamental forces that exist beyond us. He sees the horse in ancient myths as elemental spirits. In the Brihadaranyaka Upanishad which states: "Dawn is the head of the sacrificial horse," he perceives the horse as "a time-symbol, besides being the whole world" (280). For within the Upanishads, considered by Hindus to contain revealed truths, the image of *Asvamedha* sacrifice is used to depict the creation of the universe. *Prajapati*, the creator, is identified with *Asva*, or the horse, and *medhya*, the sacrifice. The horse, being a substratum for demons, gods, and humans, is used to symbolize Prajapati, the substratum of the whole universe.

Jung speaks of numerous myths in which the horse represents a tree, including the tree of death, and leads the way to the other world, as when "the souls of the dead are fetched by horsewomen, the Valkyries" (281). In Norse mythology, Valkyries are female warlike virgins who, mounted on horses, decide who will live and die in battle. They then bring half of those who die to their god Odin's afterlife hall, Valhalla, and half to the goddess Freyja's afterlife field, Folkvangr.

For Jung, "the horse is dynamic and vehicular power: it carries one away like a surge of instinct,"[4] a power widely reflected in mythic journeys across diverse cultures throughout the ages. As an animal, it represents the lower part of the human body and the impulses that arise from there, as in the Greek mythical centaurs with human upper-bodies and horse lower-bodies. As a beast of burden, it is related to the mother archetype and stands for life in its origin, as in the Greek mythical Trojan horse. With its speed, the horse signifies wind and symbolizes the libido, as mythic horses carry wild huntsmen in lustful pursuits of maidens.

Clearly, the horse is an archetype embedded in folk-memory, symbolically linking day and night, light and darkness, and life and death in continuous manifestation, or life, continuity, and time itself, as it forcefully darts into the depths of the underworld and then soars into the celestial heavens above.[5] Charging forth as swift as the wind, horses appear in myths carrying son gods, such as Surya of India and Dazhbog of Russia,[6] connecting them with fiery solar powers and life symbols, such as light, dynamic power, strength, gallantry, and mightiness.

White horses ridden by heroes in many myths represent intellect, purity, innocence, and life. For example, Buddha leaves his home on a white horse.[7] Also, "Kalki, a white horse, is to be the last incarnation or vehicle of Vishnu when he appears for the tenth time" (86). As the color white connotes transcendent perfection in many cultures, white horses often carry the archetype of hope and salvation.

Standing strong, running free, transporting warriors, heroes, gods, goddesses, and kings, the horse is highly symbolic of everything from thunderbolts and sexual organs to trees, wind, waves, and time, and plays myriad roles in dreams, myths, and folklore across all boundaries of time and place, touching human hearts and souls, igniting spiritual inspiration, and lifting the human spirit.

## Personal Horse Archetypes

Personal horse archetypes arise from our encounters with living horses, horse tales, childhood romances with carousel- and rocking horses, and the ideas and feelings about horses that permeate our culture. For example, living within the ancient Greek culture that honors many horse gods and goddesses, our personal horse archetype might be majestic, godlike, and magical like the white-winged Pegasus. Living with farm horses in England during World War I, however, our horse archetype might be of enduring friendship and loyalty, as portrayed in the twenty-first century stage production and film *War Horse* based on Michael Morpurgo's 1982 novel[8] about a farm boy who longs to reunite with his beloved horse.

## Collective Horse Archetypes

Universal horse archetypes in the collective unconscious reflect wide-ranging human experiences with horses that include their roles in drawing the carriages of kings and queens in ceremonial processions, pulling ploughs on farms, carrying soldiers in battle during wars, as well as magically romping through dreams and myths carrying the human spirit with them. Engaging the equine images grounds us in our roots and rhythms in the natural world and carries us away like wild stallions into the Otherworld. As our encounters with horses, horse tales, and imagery change, our personal and collective, or universal, archetypes change as well, as a look at the horse myths of many cultures reveal.

## Notes

1 D. Stephenson Bond, *Living Myth: Personal Meaning as a Way of Life* (Boston: Shambhala, 1993), 1. Further references to this work appear parenthetically in this work.

2 Carl. G. Jung, *Symbols of Transformation: An Analysis of a Prelude to a Case of Schizophrenia*, Bollingen Series XX (NY: Pantheon, 1956), 277. Further references to this work appear parenthetically in this work.

3 Michael Vannoy Adams, *The Mythological Unconscious* (London: H. Karnac, 2001),174. Further references to this work appear parenthetically in this work.

4 Carl G. Jung, *Dreams*, trans. R.F.C. Hull (Bollingen Series XX. Princeton: Princeton UP, 1974), 107. Further references to this work appear parenthetically in this work.

5 Jean Chevalier and Alain Gheerbrant, *The Penguin Dictionary of Symbols*, trans. John Buchanan-Brown (NY: Penguin, 1996), 516-525. Further references to this work appear parenthetically in this work.

6 Tamra Andrews, *Dictionary of Nature Myths* (Oxford: Oxford UP, 1998), 93. Further references to this work appear parenthetically in this work.

7 J. C. Cooper, *An Illustrated Encyclopaedia of Traditional Symbols* (NY: Thames and Hudson, 1979), 85. Further references to this work appear parenthetically in this work.

8 Michael Morpurgo, *War Horse* (London: Egmont, 1982). Further references to this work appear parenthetically in this work.

# CHAPTER 3

# Horses in Ancient Greek and Celtic Mythologies

As long as horses have carried humans on their backs, humans have carried forth inspirational stories of horses. The steeds' beauty, strength, and elegance are part of the human narrative, making the horse an intrinsic part of our history. Accordingly, horses are central to ancient Greek and Celtic cultures and populate their myths. Among the magical horses in Greek mythology is the mythical white-winged horse Pegasus. In Celtic mythology, with its goddess Epona, protector of horses, horses carry off the dead to the Otherworld. This chapter presents these transformative tales from ancient Greek mythologies and Celtic lore.

## Ancient Greek Mythological Horses

In ancient Greek mythology, winged horses like mighty birds draw chariots of the gods who raise the sun into the skies, watch over the earth, and sail across the heavens. They become comrades of their beloved charioteers, championing their causes, and mourning their injuries and deaths. Myths about a few of these magical steeds follow.

## Pegasus

The mythical white-winged horse Pegasus represents the passage from one plane to another. With his ascent from blood and sea foam to the realm of the immortals, the dashing white-winged horse symbolizes transformation and spiritual energy as he soars across the skies towards the heavens. According to ancient Greek mythology, he is born of the sea god Poseidon and the gorgon Medusa. When the majestic Pegasus is born, thunder and lightning pierce the skies giving him heavenly powers. Pegasus ends up on Mount Olympus serving Zeus with his thunder- and lightning-magical powers, and then as a constellation in the night sky. Children of all ages who seek to follow the mysterious stars of their imaginations can look up at him for inspiration.

Pegasus' life story begins with the powerful sea-god Poseidon shape-changing into the form of a horse, making love to the beautiful gorgon Medusa, and consummating their relationship in the temple of Athena, the shrine of the goddess of war who sprang from Zeus' head. Athena, enraged at having her temple defiled, turns Medusa's lovely curls into live snakes and makes her face so hideous that anyone who looks upon her is cast into stone. As a result, Medusa becomes a cruel monster, merciless to everyone but the Gorgons with whom she comes to live. Later, the hero Perseus slays and decapitates the monster Medusa. With that, the white-winged horse Pegasus emerges from the blood that drips down from her neck into the sea foam.

Athena takes the new magical white-winged horse Pegasus to Mount Helicon to be raised by the Muses. One day the muses begin to sing, and the mountain, filled with ecstasy, begins rising to the heavens. Under Poseidon's command, Pegasus' hoof kicks and stops the mountain's upward progress. A cool sweet stream of water called the *Fountain of Hippocrene*, or Fountain of the Horse, springs forth. Drinking the lovely water brings new soulful songs to the Muses' lips and fills their hearts with beauty. Believing the fountain to be sacred, muses flock to the water for musical and poetic inspiration. According to legend, the birth of both wine and art occurs when Pegasus' hoof unleashes the sacred spring of the Muses.

The act of Pegasus striking the fountain with his hoof thereby allowing water to gush forth is symbolic, for in this act the horse's foot becomes the dispenser of the fruitful moisture, with *fruitfulness* a symbol of one who promotes growth. The prospect of spiritual fruitfulness is worthy of highest aspirations. For many, it is actually a vital necessity.

Soon Bellerophon, prince of Corinth, desires to ride the magnificent yet untamable Pegasus, but cannot. Every time he approaches the magical steed, Pegasus gallops away. With the advice of a seer, Bellerophon visits Athena who gives him a bridle to capture and tame Pegasus. Finally able to ride the flying horse, Bellerophon slays Chimera, a hybrid monster that breathes fire. Then deciding he wants to become a god, Bellerophon mounts Pegasus and heads for Mount Olympus. With this, Zeus sends a gadfly to sting Pegasus, causing him to throw Bellerophon to the ground, doomed to wander the earth, lame and blind, until he dies alone.

Pegasus lives the rest of his days in Mount Olympus in the presence of the gods. He is entrusted with bringing lightning and thunderbolts to the powerful Zeus. Today, the magical horse, linked to the innocent child archetype that fearlessly soars and the mother archetype that dispenses water providing nourishment for the muses' souls, is honored for his earthly and heavenly deeds as a constellation in the sky, inspiring artists and dreamers to reach for the stars.

## Demeter

Widely regarded as the great Earth Goddess, Demeter is known as the mare-headed patroness of the pre-Hellenic horse cult. She is also known for being Persephone's mother by Zeus, and for her particular maternal response to Persephone's abduction and rediscovery for which she demonstrates aspects of the mother archetype. In some myths while in search of her daughter, Demeter takes the form of a horse mingling with other horses to hide from Poseidon who seeks to rape her. While she is grazing among other horses, Poseidon sees her, shape-shifts into a stallion, and mounts her. As a result, Demeter is impregnated and gives birth to the sacred horses Arion and Despoina, with Arion being the immortal horse owned by Hercules and later given to Adrastos, king of Argos, and Despoina being known as the Mistress. Mythological horses such as these are sacred to the moon because their hooves make moon-shaped marks.[1]

## Trojan Horse

Greek myths also speak of the 1184 B.C.E. Trojan War, the theme of Virgil's great poem of antiquity, *Aeneid,* as mentioned in Homer's *Odyssey.* According to myths that change in the telling, after a lingering ten-year siege, the Greeks build a hollow wooden horse of huge proportion. While their foes, the Trojans, are asleep, Greek soldiers dart inside the hollow wooden horse and hide. The Greeks then give the giant wooden horse to the Trojans, allegedly as a peace offering.

Considering their gift horse a trophy, the Trojans drag the now legendary Trojan Horse inside their city walls. At once, the Greek soldiers enclosed in the horse's body sneak out, open the city gates to their friends, and allow their compatriots to capture Troy in a decisive victory. With the Trojan Horse's birth-giving function is an obvious connection with the mother archetype, as the enclosed ovum and giver of life.

## Centaurs

The centaurs, creatures that are half-man and half-horse and better at mastering than taming their instincts, are also part of Greek mythology. Born of Ixion, king of the Lapiths, and Nephele, a cloud formed in Hera's image, they represent humankind's animal and spiritual natures, and the conflict between these opposites, or the struggle within human hearts between good and evil, self-control and wild abandon, and forgiveness and revenge.

Living in herds on Mt. Pelion in Thessaly, Greece, they dally about drunk, strike up brawls and battles, ravage crops, and rape women, demonstrating an archetype of hedonism. In Greek literature and art, they often appear pulling the chariot of Dionysus, God of wine and ecstasy, or being ridden by Eros, God of love, due to their lustful ways. Only as a result of the ancients' fondness for horses have these unruly creatures been assigned good traits.

The only immortal centaur is Chiron, known for his exceptional goodness and wisdom, who teaches Achilles, a Greek hero of the Trojan War and the central character and greatest warrior of Homer's *Iliad.* When a fight erupts between Heracles and the centaurs, Chiron is accidentally wounded. Being immortal, he is destined to live forever in terrible pain. Instead, he relinquishes his gift of immortality to Prometheus, who has given humans the gift of fire. He then dies in peace.[2] Chiron is known as the archetype of the wounded healer, referring to those who, in the process of healing from pain, learn to have compassion and empathy towards others.

# Hippogriff

Like the mythical centaurs, the magical Hippogriff's lower-body is that of a horse, but instead of having the upper-body of a human, it has the head, front legs, and wings of an eagle or fabulous mythical griffin. The term *Hippogriff* comes from the Greek word *hippo* meaning "horse" combined with the Italian word *Grifo* meaning "griffin" and has come to symbolize the impossible. The Hippogriff is also a symbol of the Greek god Apollo.

In medieval legends, Hippogriffs can fly as fast as lighting and, therefore, are usually the steeds of knights and sorcerers. In 1516, Ludovico Ariosto composes the poem "Orlando Furioso" about the fanciful creature. Then in 1824, Louis-Edouard Rioult depicts a scene from that poem in his painting "Roger Delivering Angelique," illustrating Ruggiero's rescue of Angelique while riding on a Hippogriff.

In the mythological world of Harry Potter, it seems that Hippogriffs can be aggressive and dangerous but can be tamed by such experts responsible for their care as Rubeus Hagrid, the Care of Magical Creatures Professor and Gamekeeper at Hogwarts School of Witchcraft and Wizardry.[3]

## Ancient Celtic Mythological Horses

In the ancient Celtic world that occupies Northern Europe beginning in roughly 750 B.C.E., mother goddesses are venerated; forests, woods, and groves are held sacred; and the sun and water, both givers and destroyers of life, are perceived as mysterious. In such a world, people believe that all aspects of nature, such as trees, rocks, and flowers, contain spirits and divine entities with which they are able to develop a rapport. The Celts' close relationship with the natural world manifests itself in their direct economic dependence upon the land with its crops and herds, in their perceived links between the earth's bounties and the supernatural—and in their myths, that come to be set down later by Roman historians and Christian priests.

In contrast to the ancient Celts' difficult lives on earth, their mythology embraces the underworld as a land of primeval innocence and happiness. Their dreams, inner lives, fears, and aspirations find expression in oral tales of magical rings, enchantment, and wizardry, tales in which a raven, serpent, and horse might become human with a single kiss.

From their deep connection to nature, emerges myths about the Goddess of Sovereignty and her representatives who shape-change from birds and animals to human forms as they test potential heroes for worthiness to rule the land. Would-be heroes, taking pathless paths out of magical forests, might meet fairies and other figures who present them with near-impossible tasks to test their strength and virtues. These myths gave rise to such traditions as the Arthurian romances—and magical mystical horses.

## White Horses

Among the notables from Celtic mythology is the legendary Anna Morgawse, sister of King Arthur and a Goddess of Sovereignty, who is associated with a *white horse* that represents the passage to the Otherworld in the Celtic tradition. The king's ceremonial alliance with the *white horse* signifies his ties to the Goddess of Sovereignty, which are paramount if he is to rule successfully. The *white horse* represents the Goddess of Sovereignty as it symbolizes transformation and the spiritual journey to the sacred realm, and commonly plays pivotal roles in Celtic legends,[4] with a *white horse* being an "image of that beauty gained when the spirit . . . controls the senses, [an image that conjures] the process of ascension, [as] all great Messianic figures ride such horses" (Chevalier and Gheerbrant 525).

## Riderless Horses

A *riderless horse* in the Celtic world is a symbol of military or spiritual triumph. While the image of the rider signifies perfect mastery of self and the powers of nature, Jung suggests that the opposite is true, that the image can express tormenting fears in the face of forces over which individuals and consciousness have no control (527). Hence, the riderless horse points to feared unconscious or nonhuman forces gaining control over consciousness.

## Epona

While most ancient Celtic deities are worshipped in specific locales, only Epona's worship is widespread in the Roman Empire between the first and third centuries A.C.E. Known as the *Great Mare* or *Divine Horse*, the horse goddess Epona is particularly worshipped by the Gauls for whom horses play a prominent role in their culture and represent wealth and success. A protector of horses and other animals, Epona is associated with prosperity and is often depicted in statuary and other artwork as a white horse or a lady riding side-saddle on a white horse, as is Rhiannon, her Welsh equivalent.

According to the ancient myths, Epona is born of a man, Phoulonios Stellas, and a mare of a divine nature. The very beautiful Epona becomes the horse goddess worshipped throughout Europe often with a statue surrounded with garlands of roses. A nature and earth goddess, she often appears with birds flying around her. A soldier's goddess, she is worshipped as a protector of cavalrymen and their mounts. A fertility goddess, she is worshipped for feeding corn or fruit to horses and their foals. Linked with fertility, she is sometimes shown with a foal running at her side.[5] Carrying a key that some believe to be to the horse stable while others, to the Otherworld, Epona is the beloved protector of horses as well as a mother goddess, giver of life, health, fertility, and plenty. Epona is the archetype of the feminine personality: nurturing, caring, relationshiporiented, and life-giving.

# Rhiannon

Closely associated with horses and widely believed to be Epona's Welsh equivalent is the Welsh goddess and Celtic goddess of the moon, Rhiannon, The Great Queen, as revealed in the Welsh legends of the Mabinogion. Hers is a sad love story. Once a beautiful woman in golden robes on a white horse in many versions, although some versions have her on a grey mare, Rhiannon rides ahead of Pwyll, King of Dyfed, with whom she is in love while betrothed to another. He catches up with her and they promise to marry. A convoluted tale has her marrying Pwyll after he wins her from her betrothed by trickery and then giving birth to a son who is killed with her being blamed erroneously for his death. After protesting her innocence in vain, she is condemned to sit on a horse for seven years telling her story to every passerby, offering to carry each on her back. Eventually, she is changed into a horse, becoming a symbol of the Underworld. She is also associated with birds whose sweet songs can awaken the dead at sea.[6]

# Inaugurations in Ulster

According to ancient Celtic Irish lore, to inaugurate the kings in Ulster, a white mare stands before the perspective king who then imitates a stallion pretending to mate with her. In this highly symbolic rite, the white mare represents the land of Ireland whose fertility is protected by her union with the perspective king. The white mare is then sacrificed, and the meat is cooked in a cauldron. The perspective king sits in the cooking cauldron, bathes in the juices, eats the meat, and drinks the broth.[7]

# Macha

In Celtic Irish lore, the wondrous supernatural mare-woman, Macha, is one manifestation of a divine goddess-triad and is associated with the mother goddess and horses. In her third and perhaps best-known identity, she is half-woman and half-horse. Her beauty attracts the wealthy Ulster farmer, Crundchu, whose wife she becomes. Against Macha's wishes at a public assembly of Ulsterians, farmer Crundchu boasts that his wife can outrun the king's fastest horses even though she is nine months pregnant. Hearing this, the king then forces the pregnant Macha to run a race against his finest horses. She pleads with the king and the crowds for a delay until after she delivers, but the king and the crowds have no mercy and would not consider a delay. Macha races and wins, but as soon as she crosses the finish line, she dies giving birth to twins and cursing the men of Ulster. From this day forward, during their times of greatest need for strength, the men of Ulster are gripped with the pangs of pain and helplessness that women experience in childbirth, a curse that remains for nine generations.[8]

## Horseman's Word

In Celtic Scottish lore, horses and ploughmen on farms join together as teams. Perhaps nowhere are horses and humans more connected. Scotland has a rich Celtic history going back over two thousand years, to a time when superstition is ubiquitous and unusual events and rituals are explained by stories passed on from teller to listener. In such a world, sturdy Clydesdale horses are harnessed to ploughs, and ploughmen participate in dark rituals thought to be secret.

In such rituals, uninitiated farmer boys who want to become ploughmen are stripped naked, interrogated, and taken into the back of the barn to meet with horses and become men. These initiates learn the "Horseman's Word" and, as new horsemen, are given a pair of horses at the rituals' end.[9] Some say the "Horseman's Word" is associated with knowledge of what scents, calming lotions, and drugs horses can tolerate. Some say it is related to witchcraft. But there is wide agreement that the "Horseman's Word" is a magic word that, when uttered, gives one power over horses. The farmer boys embody the archetype of the initiate willing to pass through arduous tasks to reach their goals; in this case, hoping to learn the "Horseman's Word".

# Mythological Sun and Water Horses

Horses carry chariots of mighty gods across the skies and seas. Magnificent, winged horses enable Helios, god of the sun, to rise from the sea at dawn and drive the golden chariot of the sun across the skies, bringing light to the world each morning.

Rising from the depths during storms, horses are connected with the solar and lunar powers of the sea and waves, in some myths becoming death symbols from pulling victims down into the depths. In Greek myths, waves are called *Horses of Poseidon*; in Celtic myths, *Horses of Manannan.*

## Sun Horses

### Helios

The ancient Greek sun god Helios drives a golden chariot led by four swift fire-breathing horses: Pyrois, Eos, Aethon, and Phelgon. Flying across the skies each day in a winged-golden bed until he reaches the ocean each evening, he bears witness to everything on earth. He is the sage or wise-old-man archetype. From his lofty vehicle, he sees everything that goes on during the day. Therefore, he becomes a tale bearer to other gods. Every night he is carried back to his starting point in a great divinely wrought cup.

### Apollo

In ancient Greek mythology, Apollo, son of Zeus and Leto, is the god of healing and music who plays a golden lyre, and a great archer who shoots far with a silver bow. Also, the god of light and the sun as well as truth, he cannot tell a lie. Some say that in association with Helios, one of his most important daily tasks is to harness his chariot with four horses and drive the sun across the sky.

## Water Horses

Black water horses, such as the kelpies of Scottish lore, induce travelers to mount them just before they dive into the depths carrying their victims with them. During thunderstorms when violently forceful waves turn dark and foreboding, kelpies' neighs bellow from beneath the depths. In the northern lands, the water horses are strong enough to break through the ice. At winter's end when the ice cracks, they rise from the water and push through the icy surface (Andrews 221). In the Celtic world, horses are associated with water and the healing spring shrines as well as with warfare, as warrior gods appear on horseback.

### The Death of Ferghus

Supernatural horses play both good and evil roles in Celtic mythology. In the tale "The Death of Ferghus," a horse emerges galloping from the sea. A death image, this multicolored horse with crimson mane, golden body, and green legs is a magical horse that carries people across the ocean to the Otherworld (Green, *Animals* 190). Seemingly demonstrating the archetype of Hermes, the Greek god of transitions and boundaries, this horse carries people away from the world they know across the boundaries of the great divide.

### Skyphios

According to ancient Greek legends, when the time comes to decide which deity will prove to be the most useful to humans and will, therefore, be the one for whom the city of Athens will be named, Poseidon and Athena compete for the honor. Poseidon, ruler of the sea, strikes the earth and produces a magnificent white horse, emblem of power and strength. Athena, goddess of wisdom, then produces an olive tree advising it will provide the city's inhabitants with shade and feed them for a lifetime. When the latter further advises that the olive tree is the symbol of peace and prosperity while the horse is an emblem of warfare, the city is duly named in her honor.

To celebrate the occasion, the people of Athens open their city gates and out dashes the grand white horse with its white mane flowing much like a boat's sail harnessing the wind at sea.

Captivated by the swift steed, the good people name it "Skyphios" or the "Ship of the Plains". From this horse, legends say, have descended all the wild horses of the world.[10]

### Poseidon

The god of the sea, god of horses, and brother of Zeus, Poseidon is one of twelve Olympian deities of the pantheon in ancient Greek mythology. The archetype of the tyrant, Poseidon commands the waves and causes springs to flow and storms to occur. With his dominion over water, including oceans, rivers, springs, and lakes, he is a terrifying god of stormy seas and thunderous waves. Poseidon appears riding both horses and horse-drawn chariots in ancient Greek mythology. In some myths he appears riding a Hippocampus that looks much like today's seahorse; in others, he appears riding a chariot pulled by a Hippocampus.

In mythology, gods and goddesses may shape-change to suit their needs and whims. Accordingly, Poseidon shape-changes into the form of a horse when he sires Pegasus and his brother Chrysaor by Medusa in Athena's temple, and again when he sires Arion and Despoina by Demeter in the form of a mare. Symbolizing the generative functions and the primeval waters where life begins, and embodying fertility, Poseidon is associated with the horse and other animals such as bulls and dolphins.

### Hippocampus

From Greek, Roman, and Phoenician mythologies arise the horse-headed, fish-tailed, and sometimes winged Hippocampus, also known in mythology as a horse sea monster or seahorse. With *Hippo* meaning horse and *kampus*, a monster that lives in the sea, the Hippocampus is most often depicted pulling the chariot of the Greek sea god Poseidon, or Neptune for the Romans. Other gods, goddesses, and sea nymphs are shown riding across the skies and seas on the back of Hippocampi, the latter representing the monster archetype, a distorted combination or exaggeration of ordinary characteristics yielding great strength and enormous capabilities.

In modern times, the mythic Hippocampus is used as a heraldic charge, commonly in the armorial bearings of people and places with maritime associations. The term *Hippocampus* is also used for major components of the brain in humans and other vertebrates, with humans and other mammals having two hippocampi, one on each side of the brain.

### Splendid Mane

The Poseidon of the Gaelic Pantheon is considered to be Ler, with *Ler* to mean "the sea." Ler has a son named Manannan mac Ler with *mac* for "son of". The son, Manannan mac Ler, is a patron of the sailors and has a wonderful horse named Splendid Mane. An example of the survivor archetype, this horse is exceptionally swift and travels with equal ease both on land and sea. Legends say that the horse Splendid Mane has a magic bridal that causes the images of the workers of evil magic to appear in a pail of water produced for the purpose. When tempests break over the sea in Ireland today, the breakers are said to be the *White Horses of Manannan mac Ler.*[11]

## Notes

1 Robert Graves, *The Greek Myths, Complete Edition* (London: Penguin Books, 1955), 62. Further references to this work appear parenthetically in this work.

2 Pierre Grimal, *The Penguin Dictionary of Classical Mythology*, trans. A.R. Maxwell-Hyslop (Oxford, England: Blackwell, 1991), 90. Further references to this work appear parenthetically in this work.

3 J.K. Rowling, "Chapter 22, Hippogriff (Year 3)," *The Serpent's Heart, Draco Malfoy Reader X* (Harry Potter and Pottermore, Pottermore Limited. Warner Bros. Ent. N.d.) Web. 18 January 2016

4 Sharynne MacLeod NicMhacha, *Queen of the Night: Rediscovering the Celtic Moon Goddess* (Boston: Weiser, 2005), 40-41. Further references to this work appear parenthetically in this work.

5 Jackson, Sophie, *The Horse in Myth and Legend* (Gloucestershire: Tempus, 2006), 33. Further references to this work appear parenthetically in this work.

6 Miranda Green, *Dictionary of Celtic Myth and Legend* (London: Thames and Hudson, 1992), 176. Further references to this work appear parenthetically in this work.

7 Miranda Green, *Animals in Celtic Life and Myth* (London and NY: Routledge, 1992), 187. Further references to this work appear parenthetically in this work.

8 T. W. Rolleston, *Celtic Myths and Legends* (NY: Dover, 1990), 179. Further references to this work appear parenthetically in this work.

9 Gilbert Summers, *Walkers Traditions of Scotland* (Cambridge: Martin Books, 1991), 132. Further references to this work appear parenthetically in this work.

10 Perrin, ed. *Horses in Myths, Legends, Folktales, and Other Ancient Stories* (Lexington, KY: Madeira, 2014), 3-9. Further references to this work appear parenthetically in this work.

11 M. Olden Howey, *The Horse in Magic and Myth* (Mineola, NY: Dover, 2002), 142-3. Further references to this work appear parenthetically in this work.

# CHAPTER 4

# Horses of Norse Mythology

With his identity protected under his wide-brimmed hat, the wise and fearsome one-eyed god Odin dashes through Norse sagas on his magical wingless eight-legged gray-horse named Sleipner. Together they fly like the wind between worlds mortal and divine. Odon's Sleipner is possibly the most beloved of all the horses in the richly-woven rough and tumbling Viking folk tales as told in the *Eddas* and other poetic sagas from the northern Scandinavian countries of Norway, Denmark, and Sweden from about 793 A.C.E. to 1066 A.C.E., and Iceland from about 800 A.C.E. In these tales, horses and their riders play vital roles. Warriors killed in battle, for example, are taken by horse-riding Valkyries to the afterlife in Odin's hall, Valhalla, or Freyja's field, Folkvangr.

Many wondrous horses from Norse mythology romp through this chapter, including the magical Sleipner, born of the stallion Svaoilfari and shape-shifter Loki in the form of a mare. Unveiled are insights into why Sleipner is gifted to Odin, God of noblemen and kings, while Thor, God of the common man, does not ride a horse.

## Valkyries Take Deceased Warriors to Valhalla

Viking tales' banter about life in *Midgard*, or Middle Earth, for people, elves, dwarfs, and animals, as well as life in *Asgard*, or Sky World, for gods and goddesses, and a rainbow bridge connecting these two worlds. Monsters such as trolls, dragons, sea serpents, and other creatures add punch to the tales, keeping tellers and listeners fearfully clutching their seats—or rolling over in laughter. But the subject of the horse-riding Valkyries is a serious one, free of gaiety.

For the most part in the Viking world, the dead are buried or cremated along with the prized possessions they take with them into the next world. To send them into their next lives, some Viking chiefs are given ship burials along with their treasures, weapons, and most-beloved dogs and horses. But for warriors killed in battle, the Vikings believe Odin, ruler of the gods, and the god of magic, poetry, and war, sends his horse-riding warrior maidens, the *Valkyries* or "Choosers of the Slain" through the skies to bring them to *Valhalla* or "Hall of the Slain", his great hall in Asgard where dead heroes feast forever at long tables.

These beautiful young women known as the Valkyries, armed in helmets, armors, and spears, search the battlefields for wounded warriors. Clad in shimmering armors, they ride majestic white-winged horses across the horizons. Crossing the skies, their shimmering armors create a light that has become known as the *Aurora Borealis* or "Northern Lights".

Inspired by this rich mythology with its horses, love intrigue, and battles, Richard Wagner composes an opera entitled "Die Walkure" or "The Valkyries" which opens in Munich in 1870. In particular, the dramatic yet subtle music known as "The Ride of the Valkyries" that introduces the third act is much appreciated and applauded. Exuberant and powerful, the opera continues to be performed in theatres across the globe. While some audiences find it astonishing and others offensive, the opera is one that audiences will find hard to forget—that is for sure!

## Wondrous Horses

Horses gallop through Norse mythology as comrades, carriers, healers, fortune tellers, and enablers. The horses Arvakr and Alsvior draw the Sun's chariot driven by Sol. The horse Alsvinder pulls the moon's chariot driven by Mani. The dazzling stallion Skinfaxi with a burning mane "draws Day across the world" to "gladden the eyes of men;" the stallion Hrimfaxi runs through the night sky and, in bringing "night for the noble gods,"[1] drizzles his spit and foam onto the earth creating dewdrops that glisten in the morning. Holfvarpnir is the horse Freyja rides across the sky and sea to other worlds. Gulltopp is the golden-maned horse of the god Heimdall, watchman of the gods who waits with his horn to announce the end of the world. Goldfaxi, the horse of the mighty stone and clay giant Hrungnir, is lost in a bet when Hrungnir, known for getting drunk, challenging gods to contests, and always losing, races him against Odin on the unbeatable Sleipner (with *Sleipnir*, an Old Norse name meaning gliding or smooth). The horse Grani, Sleipner's descendant, is very fine, as are other horses that colorfully abound throughout the Norse myths, but none are as fine as the eight-legged Sleipner.

## Why Sleipner Is Gifted to Odin

The Norse gods in the realm of Asgard feel vulnerable without a wall around their home to protect them from their foes. When a horseman stops by and offers to build a wall around their home within eighteen months for a high price, Loki strikes a deal. The horseman asks for the beautiful goddess Freyja's hand in marriage, the sun, and the moon in exchange for building the wall within eighteen months' time, a price to which Loki agrees only if the wall is completed within six months, not eighteen. Thinking the timeframe impossible, Loki expects to end up with half the wall without having to pay any price at all.

With the help of his horse, the horseman nearly completes the wall within the approaching six-month deadline. Odin, upset knowing that Freyja cannot marry this stranger and that life will not be worth living without the sun and the moon, begs Loki to do something. Aware the job cannot be completed without the horse's help, Loki shape-changes into a mare able to lure the horseman's horse away.

Knowing he cannot finish the wall without the help of his horse, the horseman throws an angry fit revealing his true identity as a giant, their foe. At once the gods beckon the mightiest among them, Thor, to pay the horseman for his work, which he does by taking his hammer to the giant's head. To make up for what he had done, Loki brings an eight-legged horse to Odin promising it will carry him through the air over land and sea to the dead and back, and will never be outpaced. Sleipner, the eight-legged horse, has never disappointed his master.

## Why Sleipner Is Eight-Legged

Many theories abound as to why the magical horse Sleipner is eight-legged. August Hunt in *The Terrible One's Horse* offers several hypotheses. Among these is the notion that the horse's eight legs replace the eight spokes of some European sun wheels, as depicted in rock carvings. Another theory is that Sleipner is linked to the shamanistic Windhorse that symbolizes the human soul, or the vehicle that transports the human soul after death. Also, since eight legs would seemingly go faster than four, having eight legs implies an ability to travel at high speeds.[2] These tales have been around a long time and as all myths do, they change in the telling. Accordingly in some versions, Sleipner is four-legged, with all four legs being split at the knee to make eight.

## Odin Rides Sleipner on Yddrasill, the Ash Tree

The eight-legged Sleipner is Odin's means of transportation for traveling throughout the cosmos. Riding like the wind between worlds mortal and divine, the magical horse often carries Odin up and down the trunk and through the branches of an ash tree. Now, this is not an ordinary ash tree by any means. This one is at the heart of the Norse spiritual cosmos and is named *Yggdrasil* after Odin and Sleipner who frequent it, with *Ygg* to mean "The Terrible One" referring to Odin, and *drasil* to mean Odin's horse, or Sleipner.

Located within Asgard, the home of the gods, Yggdrasil, the ash tree or tree of life, connects the nine worlds in Norse cosmology. The tree's branches extend out over the nine worlds and up to the heavens above. Having huge roots, one in Asgard, one in the land of the giants, and a third close to a well, the tree is nourished from many sources.

Odin sacrifices himself on this very tree on his quest to understand the ultimate mysteries, the wisdom of the dead. This type of sacrifice is not new to Odin who previously sacrifices one of his eyes at a well on a quest for wisdom. At the ash tree Yggdrasil, Odin hangs himself for nine days and nights, wounded with a spear. He is left to die and, thereby, learn the secrets of the dead.[3] At the end of the ninth night, however, he perceives shapes and secrets from the depths below and now equipped with new knowledge, lives on to wield new powers.

## Why Thor Does Not Ride a Horse

While Odin is the ruler of the gods and thereby fully deserving of the finest horse according to Norse mythology, Thor, or Thunderer, son of Odin and Freyja and god of the household and common folk who marries Sif, a peasant, is deemed less worthy. Therefore, the Mighty Thor, hammer-carrying protector of Midgard, rides a battle-chariot drawn not by the horses of Odin's station in that mythical world, but goats.

**Notes**

1 Kevin Crossley-Holland, *The Norse Myths* (NY: Pantheon, 1980), 76. Further references to this work appear parenthetically in this work.

2 August Hunt, *The Terrible One's Horse: Revealing the Secrets of Norse Myth* (Stag Spirit Books, 2012), 25. Further references to this work appear parenthetically in this work.

3 David A. Leeming, *The Handy Mythology Answer Book* (MI: Visible Ink, 2015), 152. Further references to this work appear parenthetically in this work.

# CHAPTER 5

# Mythological Horse Tales from Asia

Human life in Asia is rich with its abundant nationalities, ethnicities, and cultures that are expressed in a wealth of mythologies and folklore, as well as music, visual arts, literature, and cuisine. The home of numerous religions and philosophies, each playing a major role in its many regions, the cultures in Asia bring a cornucopia of stories to life, a few of which follow.

## Hindu Mythological Horses

From India in South Asia is Hinduism, a way of life, or *dharma*, with belief systems, traditions, rituals, and ethics that are as meaningful and relevant today as they were thousands of years ago. According to Hindu beliefs, each soul experiences many lives. For after the death of one body, or *incarnation*, the soul is reborn into a new living body. This cycle applies not only to the individual souls of humans, but to animals and all species, even the universe which has been in a continual process of decay and renewal for millions of years. In a seemingly endless cycle or cosmic dance, every individual is responsible for following their own pattern, or *dharma*. From these beliefs, myths and tales of gods, goddesses, and horses abound.

Key to much of Hindu mythology is the battle with the forces of nature as well as between deities and demons, in which the deities must win, so that the kingdom of the gods and goddesses can be retained and restored, and the proper socioeconomic order predicated on the myths' tenets can remain intact and go unchallenged. Read, told, enacted, dramatized, and danced again and again for the young and old throughout the ages, Hindu mythologies provide enduring wisdoms to which generations of people turn. In story form, they portray guidelines by which people live. The characters in the stories or mythologies become heroes and role models that people might choose, or be advised, to emulate. Some of these myths, and associated rituals, involve a horse.

## Terra-Cotta Horse

The earliest Hindu scriptures, the Vedas, present hymns that describe rituals, some of which include animal sacrifice. Now, with an appreciation for and valuing of nonviolence, not all Hindus are in favor of animal sacrifices, yet the rituals are part of Hindu history and lore. In this lore, the horse is ranked among the greatest of the animal victims.[1]

As the tale unfolds, the Madurai region houses many temples that are dedicated to Aiyanar, the Tamil village god, and provides shrines to the little deity Karuppan. While Aiyanar is the master over his servant Karuppan, the latter oversees the temple from his place at the edge of the site. It happens that Aiyanar's favorite gift is a terra-cotta horse which reflects his station in life as it is associated with kings in India. As a result, he is given a terra-cotta horse, but when he is given one, another must be given to Karuppan according to long-standing traditions, as both preside over the temple.

The problem with this is that Karuppan, thought to have been a former evil spirit, favors animal sacrifice. Therefore, when the horse is offered at the shrine of Aiyanar, who favors vegetarianism, the shrine is shielded from the horse killing, or the sacrifice (90). The myth changes with each teller and telling, as do discussions on the valuing of higher and lower deities and of animal sacrifice and nonviolence, including vegetarianism.

## Horses in Hindu Mythology

In Hinduism, animals such as the horse are a vibrant part of everyday life as well as their mythology. Surya, the Sun god in Hindu mythology, journeys through the sky each day on a chariot drawn by seven horses named Gayatri, Brhati, Usnik, Jagati, Tristup, Anustup, and Pankti. The seven horses, or, alternatively, one horse with seven heads in some versions, represent the seven colors of the rainbow or sunlight, the seven days of the week, and the seven chakras in the human body.

Hindus revere many divinities in animal form, and animals serve as symbols. Among the Vedas' many references to animals is the horse. A white-winged horse, for example, emerges from churning ocean waters and is taken to Indra, the leader of the gods, who removes its wings to confine its movement and gives it to humans for their welfare. Many stories about Lord Indra and the snowy-white horse are threaded throughout Hindu mythology. Some versions follow.

## Uchaishravas

Within Hindu mythology is the story of Uchaishravas, a snowy-white flying horse with seven heads that emerges from devas' and demons' churning of the milky ocean. Considered among the best of horses, when the fabulous snowy-white seven-headed horse appears, Lord Indra, who in Vedic times is the supreme ruler of the gods and leader of the Devas, as well as being the god of war, thunder, and storms, claims the snowy-white horse and rides him. With that, Uchaishravas becomes known as Lord Indra's *vahana* or "vehicle".

The legend of Uchaishravas' rising from the milky ocean is told in the Vishnu Purana, Ramayana, and more, including the Bhagavad Gita, which is part of the Mahabharata. The many tales about Uchaishravas include one that occurs in the twelfth century in which the creator-god performs a sacrifice out of which rises the white-winged horse, Uchaishravas. In another tale, Uchaishravas rises again out of the milky ocean and is taken by the king of the demons to help him attain many impossible things. In other tales, when Prithu is installed as the first king on earth, Uchaishravas is made the king of the horses.

In the Mahabharata is a discussion about the color of Uchaishravas' tail. One character says it is white while another, black. The loser in this debate is to become the servant of the winner, so to win the debate, the one who says it is black asks her son to cover the tail to make it appear black. As a result, the latter wins the debate and gains a servant.

# Buddhist Mythological Horses

The Buddha, Siddhartha Gautama, is said to have been born in the Year of the Horse, with the horse being one of the twelve animals in the Asian sixty-year calendar. Although Buddha first walked the earth twenty-five thousand years ago, Buddhism continues to be compelling and relevant for people today. Founded in the late 6th century B.C.E. by Siddhartha Gautama, known as the Buddha, Buddhism is an important religion not only in most countries of Asia but, with its migration to the West, in many corners of the world. Promoting the brotherhood of all beings, the Buddhist vision is that everything in the universe depends on everything else. Buddhism teaches that awareness is achieved through liberation. Seeing all beings as Buddha beings, Buddhism teaches, "The task is only to know what is, and then to act in relation to the brotherhood of all of these beings," such that the powers that animate people also animate the life of the world. Thus, people need not dominate, subjugate, or control nature, but instead live in accord with it.[2]

## Full Awakening: Bodhi and Bodhisattvas

To live in harmony with nature is central to Buddhist practice. Joseph Campbell affirms, "The Orient calls *bodhi*: full awakening to the crystalline purity of the bed or ground of one's own and the world's true being."[3] The image evokes that of a perfectly transparent crystal that is there, yet as though not there; all things, when seen through it, can become luminous in its light.

The word *bodhisattva* comes from the Sanskrit roots *Bodhi* meaning "awakening" or "enlightenment", and *sattva* meaning "sentient being" with etymological roots that include "intention" and "courage" or "heroism".[4] Tibetan Buddhists, for example, refer to bodhisattvas as "awakened warriors" for they manifest great strength of character and virtue for the sake of others, and they are not merely archetypes, they are "great cosmic beings, helping us all to become bodhisattvas" (306). They are ordinary beings, making their way back to Buddha, or to the one who waked up, according to Campbell, who suggests that everyone is a manifestation of Buddha consciousness whether or not they are aware of it, and each has the potential to wake up to their Buddha consciousness within (Campbell, *Power* 57).

Bodhisattvas are ever present, for everyone has the capacity to be a bodhisattva. Through stories of modern exemplars of the bodhisattva archetype, the archetypal qualities of bodhisattva compassion emerge. Yet the fullness of the qualities transcends the stories and definitions attached to the figures. For the aim of awakening practice is to go beyond the stories and definitions; it is to become true to the openness and wonder of our lives, and our intimate connection to all beings.

Buddhist liberation is about fully knowing our stories and not being trapped by them. We each contain multitudes of stories, including stories about bodhisattvas, and about awakening from stories (Leighton 308). Awakening to the suchness of reality helps enable us to awaken to the interconnectedness of all beings. The crucial vow of bodhisattva practice is just to continue to awaken and care for all beings, as the following horse tales reveal.

### Kanthaka

In this myth, Kanthaka, the white horse of Prince Siddhartha, the buddhisattva or Future Buddha, is with Prince Siddhartha in all major Buddhist events prior to the latter's renunciation of the world. Suddenly everything takes a turn. Prince Siddhartha enters the homeless path of the nameless anonymous ascetic, severs his hair, exchanges his garments for the robe of the ascetic beggar, and dismisses his faithful charioteer, but not before asking him to inform his parents that he is doing well. Meanwhile his white horse Kanthaka, standing by and listening, is unable to bear his grief at the thought, "I shall never see my master anymore," and dies of a broken heart. The horse is then reborn as the god Kanthaka in the Heaven of the Thirty-Three Gods.[5]

Here, the horse is the symbol of the bodily vehicle; the rider, the spirit. When the latter comes to an end of its reincarnations, the vehicle necessarily dies. With a deep empathy for the animal's feelings, the horse's discreet protest and sadness are expressed.

*White Horse Monastery*

The white horse plays an important role in Chinese Buddhism as this legend reveals. In the year 63 A.C.E., the Chinese emperor Ming-ti has a vision of a man pointing west while announcing to him the appearance in the world of a Perfect Man. Impressed by this vision, the emperor sends a team of eighteen men to go west to find him.

While on their way, the men meet two men holding a white horse laden with books, images, and relics. Seeing the white horse, they realize the men are those they are seeking and bring them to Loyang, the home of the Hans emperor, to be installed into the White Horse Monastery, the earliest Buddhist sanctuary in China.

*Cloud, or Valahaka*

In the Buddhist tradition, the bodhisattva Avalokiteshvara, who embodies the compassion of all Buddhas, is a polyvalent character like Vishnu possessed by divine powers and able to take many forms. He may become a person or may, as an animal, appear as a fabulous, winged horse named Cloud or Valahaka, carrying the Buddha away to safety. Sometimes male and other times female, he or she possesses divine powers and assumes the manifestations needed to help living beings reach enlightenment.

*Hayagriva*

Avalokiteshvara (*Hayagriva* in Sanskrit, *Ba-to Kwan-non* in Japanese) is often depicted with a horse's head in his headdress and a scowl that incites awakening. Horse-headed Hayagriva is thought to embody the speech aspect of all Buddhas. His high-pitched whinny, perceived as the cry of wisdom, cuts through illusion and false attachments, evoking the nature of reality, the enlightened mind.

Further, the white horse tradition reaches Japan where the horse's head in Ba-to's hair must be white to be effective. In Japan, Ba-to Kwan-non is represented with an angry expression and a third eye in his forehead, with a horse's head protruding from hair that stands upright. Often there are three heads, one on either side of the central head with differing angry expressions, and above the central head is the head of a horse.

In Tibet, Ba-to, the horse-headed Kwan-non, takes the form of the Tibetan masculine divinity Hayagriva and remains the Goddess of Mercy for the common people.[6] Horse dealers in Tibet worship the patron god of horse dealers as the Protector of Horses that neighs like a horse and, thus, frightens away demons. Since he neighs to announce his coming, his headdress is marked with a horse's head. Therefore, he becomes known as the horse-necked one.

### Windhorse

In the Tibetan Buddhist traditions of East and Central Asia, the term *windhorse* is used to express the concept of riding the wind, with *wind* to mean the breath needed for sustaining life and *horse*, the riding, or the energy of the breath and life; it also refers to flags blowing in the wind. Used primarily for the colorful flags blowing in the winds of Tibet, windhorse has its origins in secular Asian folk cultures but has become associated with Buddhism. While the term in Tibetan culture conjures up the display of brightly colored prayer flags placed in close proximity to sacred sites in the Tibetan world, it actually has a deeper meaning. Windhorse refers to the experience of riding the horse of our lives, or the letting go of the worries and obstacles that hold us back.

Besides being the term used for colorful flags blowing in the wind, windhorse is a spiritual principle. This is the notion of Buddhist awakened nature, of the inseparability of wisdom and compassion. Standing for the concept of goodness, the balance of openness and gentleness, as well as non-violent courage and fearlessness, *windhorse*, to mean riding the wind, is a symbol for the idea of well-being or good fortune.

## Buddhism: Promotes Reverence for Life

Buddhism, compared to a beneficent rain that nourishes all beings, offers possibilities for humans to interconnect with all that is, which includes the natural environment in which they live. Poet Gary Snyder, author of the popular poem "Hay for the Horses" (1959) that sheds light on the value of setting goals before life passes by, recalls the ancient Buddhist precept, "Cause the least possible harm," and the implicit ecological call to "Let nature flourish"[7] in his support of a reverence for life, human and otherwise. Snyder, a student of Zen and a Pulitzer Prize-winning poet, refers to the Buddhist teachings of impermanence, suffering, compassion and wisdom in promoting mindful living the Buddhist way, which cultivates a human-nature relationship that is fundamentally ecological.

## Horse Tales from Japan

Human and horse bonds in Japan are deep, as the following Japanese myth, or tale parents might read to their children, illustrate. The Zen Buddhist artist Sesshu, living from 1420 to 1506, "painted animals that were so real that, according to legend, they came to life."[8] To punish Sesshu as a young boy for drawing instead of meditating, senior monks bind him so tightly that tears like dripping paint stream down his cheeks into puddles onto the ground. Dipping into the paint-like puddles with his fingers that are free, Sesshu paints a rat on the ground. Upon completion, the rat comes to life, scurries over to him, and chews the ties that bind him. From this, the masters allow Sesshu to paint whenever he likes.

One day he paints a horse on a sliding glass door. Each night coming to life, the horse darts through the village to a garden of carrots that he eats. When the sun rises, the farmer sees the missing carrots and the hoof prints that lead not to the many grazing horses, but to Sasshu's painting. After being enraged for days, the farmer revisits the painting only to find carrot greens hanging from the horse's mouth and mud on his hoofs. Getting a bright idea, he asks Sesshu to paint a halter on the horse and a post nearby. Soon, the horse is tied to the post and the carrots are no longer eaten.

## Horse of Bronze

Riding through the streets during the festival of the *Minige*, or "The Body Escaping," is Oho-kuninushi, Deity of Kitzuki on the Bronze Horse.[9] Part of the festival, the rite is so mysterious that only after his death is the officiating priest able to tell his son about it by means of his deceased man's spirit. This rite is similar to the following three. The first is the great carved wooden dragon that would run atop the roofs of many houses disturbing their residents until his wooden throat is cut and he becomes a work of art. The second is the bronze deer that would run through the streets at night disturbing citizens until his head is cut and his visits end. The third is the gigantic tortoise of stone nearly sixteen feet high that would swim across a pond covered with lotus until his ability is curtailed. The outcome for Oho-kuninushi, Deity of Kitzuki on the Bronze Horse is no different. This, like all myths, changes in the reading and telling, showing the human imagination's engagement with horses.

## Chinese Horse Tale

For thousands of years the following Chinese tale has been kindling wonder within imaginative minds and hearts. "The Magic Stallion" is a magical story about the wooden stallion of a carpenter set up to compete at the Royal Palace against the iron fish of a blacksmith as a means to demonstrate which master craftsman has the superior skill, the carpenter or the blacksmith. The wooden stallion is presented to show how it can fly faster than a bird, easily taking a person around the world, while the iron fish is presented to show how it can swim seven seas with a hundred thousand sacks of rice on its back. Watching, the prince, the emperor's youngest son, insists upon riding the wooden stallion.[10]

The wooden stallion and the prince take off, ending up in a new city where they come across the most beautiful girl in the world whose father, this city's emperor, has the gods build a castle in the sky to house and protect his daughter from onlookers. The wooden stallion lifts the prince up to the castle in the sky where he meets and instantly falls in love with the princess and, secretly, stays with her all night. When her father, the emperor, discovers that a man has been with his daughter, he has her furniture painted and sends out scouts to look for the man with paint on his clothes.

The prince hears about this, notices paint on his clothes from the girl's furniture and throws his clothes out of a window. The clothes land onto a poor old man who thinks they come from heaven and puts them on. He is seized, jailed, and about to be hanged for the crime of being with the Emperor's daughter when the prince confesses to spare the old man's life and then mounts his wooden stallion and flies straight to the princess's castle to ask the princess to go with him to his parent's kingdom. She agrees and together they mount the wooden stallion and dash off. Suddenly the princess realizes she left without the jewelry she had promised her mother she would give her husband's parents after she marries, and cries until the prince sends her back to her castle on the wooden stallion while he waits there.

When she returns to her castle, her father seizes and imprisons her and the wooden stallion. Meanwhile the prince wanders aimlessly, being completely lost without her. One thing leads to another and finally the prince and princess are reunited under false pretenses. The wooden stallion is the hero as without the horse to carry them back to the safety of the prince's parent's kingdom, the prince and princess would never be able to marry and live happily ever after together. In the end, the carpenter is rewarded by the prince's father, the emperor, for crafting the wooden stallion that enables his son to explore the world and find his beloved princess.

## Korean Horse Tale

In the story of the kingdom of Silla within Korean mythology is a huge white horse. The story unfolds with the people in the kingdom gathering to pray for a king. Suddenly, as if by magic or as an answer to their prayers, a huge white horse arises from a lightning bolt and bows to a shining egg. The great white horse then flies back to heaven and, lo and behold, the eggshell breaks open and out pops the boy, Park Hyeokgeose. The people's prayers are truly answered. This boy grows up to be king and unites six warring states. Hyeokgeose of Silla is the founding monarch of Silla, one of the three kingdoms of Korea.

Another version of the same story specifies that in 69 B.C.E., when the heads of the six chiefdoms gather together to discuss forming a kingdom and selecting a king, suddenly a strange light shines down from the sky over a well in the forest where a white horse is bowing down. At that well, Chief Sobeolgong of Goheo discovers a large egg. Out of the egg comes a boy whose body, when bathed, radiates light in which birds and beasts dance. The Chief raises the boy who is revered by six chieftains. When the boy is thirteen, the chieftains make him king and he marries Lady Alyeong who is said to have been born from a dragon's ribs.

## Horse Tale from the Philippines

Those traveling to the mountains and forests of the Philippines better be forewarned. They could happen upon a Tikbalang, one of those benevolent mythical human-horses known to lurk in the mountains and forests of the Philippines. Travelers who chance upon one probably do not expect to see the tall mythical creature with his horse-like animal head and feet, and surprisingly long limbs on his human-like body. Some think these creatures might be aborted fetuses that have been transformed and sent down to earth.

Travelers must be careful not to disturb the Tikbalang if they should chance upon him. For if the truth be known, they do not like to be disturbed. Also, they like to protect their entire kingdom from being disturbed. So, travelers who come upon a Tikbalang would be wise to stay clear of him and not cause a disturbance.

According to the lore of the land, the playful creatures seem to get a kick out of leading travelers astray. Wisdom from the common lore indicates that Tikbalangs can shape-change into human forms, likely those of victims' acquaintances such as relatives whose voices and mannerisms they assume. The victims may think they are following their relatives into the woods, when in reality they are following transformed Tikbalangs who may never let them see the light of day again. Further, some say Tikbalangs can become invisible to the human eye. Other wisdom indicates that by plucking three golden hairs from a Tikbalang's mane before he can eat the traveler or victim ensures that the creature will serve the traveler forevermore.

## Vietnamese Horse Tale

More than one white horse myth dignifies Vietnamese folklore which is filled with many myths of powerful spirits exerting power in the region. One story begins after Vietnam becomes independent from China in the eleventh century. The king leaves Hanoi and, for a year and a half, tries to build walls for a new citadel. But the land is marshy and the walls collapse. He makes offerings to the spirits and then in a dream a white-haired man appears before the king and bows, saying he wants long life for the king and the empire.

While praying, the king is dazzled by the sight of a great white horse galloping west from the temple and leaving hoof prints which are considered good luck. The king understands the horse as an incarnation of the river god and takes it as an omen to build the citadel on the ground marked with the hoof prints. Accordingly, the citadel is built and remains intact. The king makes the white horse the spirit of the citadel, believing it will look after the country. To this day, the White Horse God is honored in the form of a life-sized wooden statue. The White Horse Temple (or Bach Ma Temple, with the Chinese terms *bach* meaning "white" and *ma* meaning "horse") at the heart of historic Hanoi recalls the folklore of the city's founding and has been standing for over a thousand years.[11]

## Horses in Ancient Persia

Dating back to the third millennium B.C.E. in ancient Persia, now Iran in Western Asia, is the home of the elegant yet spirited Caspian horses so prized today in American and other equestrian societies. The regal horses disappear from sight when Muslims conquer Persia in 627 A.C.E. They do not reappear until 1965 when Louise Firouz, an American teaching horseback riding to children in Tehran, rediscovers a small group of them near the Caspian Sea and exports some to other lands.[12] From Iran comes the heartwarming myth of Qeytas, a Caspian colt that not only jumps far as do most Caspian's, but flies and talks—enabling him to save a prince.

## Qeytas, an Iranian Colt

When the prince's father the king remarries after the prince's mother dies, the new queen wants to kill the prince allowing her own children to inherit the throne. Each time she tries to poison or trap the prince, Qeytas-the-colt warns him. Finally, the frustrated new queen announces she wants to make a soup of the prince's colt-friend Qeytas, an idea to which the prince agrees only if he is granted one last ride on Qeytas' back.

Off they fly, never to return. They land in another kingdom where the prince disguises himself as a poor gardener boy. Taking a ride on Qeytas to ease his loneliness, the prince is seen by a princess who falls in love with him with a thousand hearts. When he returns to his disguise, she finds and recognizes him.

Soon the time comes for this kingdom's king to look for suitors for his three daughters. The first two settle on sons of the king's wazir, or prime minister. The third and youngest daughter, whose heart belongs to the prince, refuses all suitors, choosing only the dirty gardener boy (who she knows is the prince). This makes the king so ill that nothing will cure him except a meal of a rare golden bird.

When the first two daughters' suitors are unable to deliver the rare bird, the prince flies off on Qeytas' back and captures the golden bird which he, in his gardening rags, delivers in a soup to the king. With one taste of the bird soup, the king is cured but enraged. With the king inflamed at his two daughters' fine suitors' failed efforts in the face of the lowly gardener boy's success, the prince throws off his gardening rags and, in royal garb, is given his beloved princess's hand in marriage. Soon the young couple rules the kingdom, giving Quetas the opportunity to come and go as he pleases (64-68).

This tender tale may stir the imaginations of everyone who hears or reads it. It offers the comforting feeling that, whether in Iran or any corner of the world, horses can speak to us, save us from assorted dangers, and carry us away to a better world. The horse in such tales is uplifting, offering us compassion, mobility—and a touch of magic.

## Notes


1 C. J. Fuller, *The Camphor Flame: Popular Hinduism and Society in India* (Princeton UP, 1992), 88. Further references to this work appear parenthetically in this work.

2 Joseph Campbell, *The Power of Myth with Bill Moyers*, ed. Betty Sue Flowers (NY: Broadway, 2001), 22-24. Further references to this work appear parenthetically in this work.

3 Joseph Campbell, *The Masks of God: Creative Mythology* (New York: Penguin Books, 1976), 66. Further references to this work appear parenthetically in this work.

4 Taigen Dan Leighton, *Faces of Compassion: Classic Bodhisattva Archetypes and Their Modern Expression* (Boston: Wisdom Publications, 2003), 26. Further references to this work appear parenthetically in this work.

5 Heinrich Zimmer, *Myths and Symbols in Indian Art and Civilization*, ed. Joseph Campbell (Bollingen Series VI. Princeton: Princeton UP, 1972), 162. Further references to this work appear parenthetically in this work.

6 Alice Getty, *The Gods of Northern Buddhism: Their History and Iconography* (NY: Dover, 1988), 94. Further references to this work appear parenthetically in this work.

7 Gary Snyder, *A Place in Space: Ethics, Aesthetics, and Watersheds* (New York: Counterpoint, 1995), vii. Further references to this work appear parenthetically in this work.

8 Gerald and Loretta Hausman, *The Mythology of Horses: Horse Legend and Lore Throughout the Ages* (NY: Three Rivers, 2003), 48. Further references to this work appear parenthetically in this work.

9 F. Hadland Davis, *Myths and Legends of Japan* (NY: Dover, 1992), 275. Further references to this work appear parenthetically in this work.

10 Isabelle C. Chang, *Chinese Fairy Tales* (NY: Shocken, 1965), 12. Further references to this work appear parenthetically in this work.

11 Barbara Cohen, "White Horse Temple," *Destinations: Vietnam / Hanoi* (ThingsAsian, 1995), Web. 17 Feb 2016.

12 Josepha Sherman, *Magic Hoofbeats: Horse Tales from Many Lands* (Cambridge, MA: Barefoot, 2004), 63. Further references to this work appear parenthetically in this work.

# CHAPTER 6

# Horse Mythologies in Monotheistic Cultures

Playing special roles in the mythologies of many cultures since ancient times, horses have been widely displayed in artwork and iconography. From the mythical white-winged horse Pegasus widely regarded as a symbol of celestial ascent to the centaurs and horse-headed fish-tailed hippocampus and beyond, horses are central to Greek culture and populate their myths. Horses are also plentiful in Celtic mythology with its goddess and protector of horses Epona. In many Asian cultures, horses have played important roles for thousands of years not only in transportation and military services and as companions and pets, but as symbols of transformation and sources of inspiration for the arts, mythology, and folklore. In some Asian cultures, the horse is regarded as sacred in association with particular deities. Yet, while symbolic horses might be less widespread in cultures with monotheistic religions, they are significant as a look at their place in Arab, Jewish, and Christian traditions and mythologies reveal.

## Horses in the Arab World

As majestic and powerful as they are, horses have never been thought to be of ordinary beginnings. Among the greatest horse people of the world, the Arabs have a version of how the superb animals originate. The first horse, they believe, is created out of a handful of the south wind by Allah, who declares:

> Thy name shall be Arabian. . .. I have preferred these above all beasts of burden in as much as I have made thy master thy

friend. I have given thee the power of light without wings, be it in onslaught or retreat. I will set [humans] on thy back that shall honor and praise Me and sing Hallaujah to My Name.[1]

In the sixth century, the Prophet Mohammed, the founder of the Islamic religion who is both a visionary and a pragmatist, ensures the spread of the breed throughout the Old World.[2] In Islam that forbids idolatry, the horse is called "the Supreme Blessing" as it brings happiness in this world and eternal reward (63). Muhammad's personal horse, named *Al Borak* meaning "lightning" in Arabic, is a mythical white-winged mare said to have a human head, thus proving the ancient metaphysical belief that horses and humans are once joined. After Muhammad's death in 632 A.C.E., his followers proclaim he is born to the Seventh Heaven on the back of Al Borak.

## Horses in Jewish Traditions

Some say the first known rider of the horse is Ishmael, son of Abraham and ancestor of the desert Bedu tribes (Macgregor-Morris 45). After the breakup of these tribes, the story of the horse continues with King Solomon who, with disregard for the Israelites' law that forbids the keeping of horses on the grounds of idolatry, encourages horse breeding.

Four sets of horses appear in the Old Testament, *Zechariah*, Chapter 6 verses 1 to 5, as follows: "And again I . . . looked, and behold, there came four chariots out from between two mountains; . . .. In the first chariot *were* red horses; and in the second chariot black horses; in the third chariot white horses; and in the fourth chariot grisled and bay horses." An angel explains, "These *are* the four winds of the heavens, which go forth from standing before the Lord of all the earth." Here, horses are thought to be patrolling life on earth to keep it peaceful. Horses also appear in the Talmud where it is said that dreams of white horses moving or not moving are good, while dreams of chestnut or dark horses are good only if the horses are not moving.[3]

Recapturing painful and joyful parts of Jewish history and culture is the twentieth-century Polish-born, Jewish-American storyteller Isaac Bashevis Singer who writes in Yiddish and is awarded the Nobel Prize in Literature for 1978. Among his prolific writings is the following horse tale.

## Naftali the Storyteller and His Horse, Sus

Naftali loves stories and, even more, loves his horse, Sus. When his family and friends tell him he cannot make a life of stories and a horse, he hitches Sus to a wagon he fills with books and embarks on a journey collecting and sharing tales.

While his life is rich and his journey rewarding, his dearest prize is his humble horse that makes his journey possible. Naftali stops inside the stables to visit Sus, his horse. To his delight, he finds Sus seemingly listening to other horses' tales and telling his own. When Sus dies, Naftali buries him, marking his grave with the oak whip he never used. Soon, the whip sprouts shoots and roots, just as his stories had done.

In this warm story of friendship and faith, Naftali and his horse share a deep bond of loving friendship and genuine concern for the other's well-being. Their faith in each other and in their ability to make their way kindles hope and optimism within us all.[4]

## Horses in Christian Mythology and Iconography

Horses are resplendent in ancient polytheistic halls and artwork. They appear in statues, tapestries, and paintings that illustrate pageants and processions featuring horses, horse riders, and horse-drawn vehicles. They are shown pulling ceremonial chariots, accompanying or carrying deities to accomplish impossible feats, or dashing to unimaginable places. While they figure wildly in today's plethora of Christmas gifts as decorations on everything from hats and purses to jewelry, tissue boxes, and tree ornaments, the history of horse images and statuary within Christian traditions is convoluted. Below is a brief look at the use of artwork and iconography in Christianity's early days showing how far the use of imagery has come—even of horses.

## Artwork and Imagery

The first Christians are called upon to paint images for Christian burial, such as the Roman catacombs. Their artwork is done not to create earthly beauty, but to show God's mercy and power. With the decline of the Roman Empire and the rise of Christianity, there is a shift away from the delicate refinement and harmony of the Greek artistry toward a more crude style.[5] In 311 A.C.E., the Emperor Constantine establishes the Christian Church as a power in the State and, with this declaration, the role of art in church buildings changes. Suddenly, churches must be able to accommodate more people, and statues are not to be permitted in churches, as they are too much like the idols that are condemned in the Bible. The belief that statues might obstruct people's ability to imagine and believe in an Almighty Invisible God prevails.

Yet at the end of the sixth century A.C.E., Pope Gregory the Great encourages the portrayals of Biblical stories as a way to share them with the masses that are illiterate. Thus, a highly restricted type of artwork is permitted, a type that begins in a basilica in Ravena, Italy in around 500 A.C.E. This artwork shows that something miraculous and sacred is happening. It is a mosaic with an unrealistic background comprised of flecks of gold from which a ceremonial Christ figure with outstretched arms and clad in a purple robe emerges. Lacking the movement and expression of Greek and Roman art, this becomes a symbol of Christ's abiding power that is embodied in the Christian church (135-136).

The sophisticated ways to create art are not lost in Christian artwork, but the purpose for which art is made in the churches is significant and impacts not only the development of art but, in the Eastern, Greek-speaking parts of the Roman Empire whose capital is Byzantium or Constantinople, the willingness to accept the Latin Pope's ideas. In 754, all religious art is forbidden in the Eastern Church where the people, known as iconoclasts, smash statues and forbid them from being in their church. For their opponents, however, the images are not only useful, but they are seen as holy and as "mysterious reflections of the supernatural worlds" (138).

Byzantine artists then create a solemn style of artwork that reflects the Greek and Roman traditions, while artists from Western traditions go down a path of more diversity and expressiveness. Moving further West in the seventh and eighth centuries, the Muslims that conquer Persia, Mesopotamia, Egypt, North Africa, and Spain, strongly forbid religious icons and images. Art, however, is not easily suppressed and comes to life not reflecting human forms as such, but imaginative patterns, as they give life to their dream worlds in lacework, lines, and color (146).

## Horse in Byzantine Iconography

Byzantine iconography refers to the distinct tradition and style of the Orthodox religious images painted during the Byzantine Empire from the fifth century to the fall of Constantinople. Its rich tradition continues today as testament to the powerful religious experience that their images evoke. On Orthodox Church walls can be seen the mysteries of the Christian faith. Examples of Orthodox Byzantine iconography include mosaics of Saint George in Battle depicting Saint George as a warrior saint riding a white horse. Honoring the son of light fighting against the dragon of darkness, the icon of Saint George teaches the faithful that evil is conquered by God's power working through those that are obedient to God's will in Christ's love.

## Horses' Presence and Absence

Icons are not merely aesthetic objects: their power is contained within the particular framework of belief and worship to which they belong. In Christian iconography, historians consider the theological arguments concerning the reconciliation of Christ's two natures, "his divinity and his humanity." They do not ponder "how images of Christ affected the way people conceptualized him, . . . but how they grasped him" and propel people well beyond ideas, for often images' power to stir emotions overwhelms the ideas they are supposed to carry (10).

The root word *eikon* from the Ancient Greeks "could mean any sort of image, [but] in the strict historical sense of the term means a wood-panel painting of a sacred object intended for veneration" (178). The special role of Christian iconography is in its cultic use, as it is not the medium that makes an icon, from paintings to frescos, but the content and how it is portrayed. The vision of the icon is spiritual; its purpose is not to capture, through the use of color, expression, and composition, the natural look of persons or objects, but their spiritual essence.

The presence and absence of the horse and the uses of the donkey, or ass, are highly significant in Christian iconography. For example, the detailed artwork that emerges from the ancient sarcophagus of the "Entry of Christ into Jerusalem" do not show horses and chariots; rather, "Christ's transport is emphasized in the images by the small stature, large head, and huge ears of the beast" (30). The lack of the horse, chariot, and other accouterments reflects Jesus of Nazareth's humble origins as a working-class carpenter, though his long robes set him apart from the crowds that wear short tunics (37-38). Importantly, "the opposition of the horse of warfare and the humble, agricultural ass is commonplace in biblical language," as he is shown seated in a feminine pose on a "farmer's ass" to demonstrate the "uselessness of imperial parades" (45).

There are many Eastern instances of "Christ riding side-saddle on the ass" which then prevail in Byzantine art. The meaning of the side-saddle pose is debated, but as "no emperor ever rode side-saddle," the pose reinforces an anti-imperial role of Christ. In Antiquity, it is commonly a woman's way of riding and is "the ultimate non-military pose"—all of which inspire ways of grasping Christ. Very significantly, "in a relief from Egypt, Christ's companions are transformed into angels, one holding the ass's bridle, while another supports Christ's blessing right arm" (3943). Clearly, "Christ's Entry with angels is his entrance in the divine liturgy" (41) with asses, not horses, being a key component in the iconography.

## Horses in the New Testament

In the New Testament are references to horses that are widely depicted in artwork. In *Revelation,* Chapter 6, verses 1 to 8 is the following:

> Then I saw the Lamb open one of the seven seals, and I heard one of the four living creatures call out, as with a voice of thunder, "Come!" I looked, and there was a white horse! [With]

the second seal, . . . out came another horse, bright red; [With] the third seal, . . . a black horse! [With] the fourth seal, . . . a pale green horse![6]

The *Four Horsemen of the Apocalypse*, with its varied interpretations, can be appreciated as an event in which the Almighty destroys the powers of evil and raises the righteous to life. In it, he has a scroll on which words are inscribed, held together by seven seals. When the first seal is broken, the four horsemen appear, each on a different colored horse. Some hold that the rider on the white horse represents conquest or the return of Jesus of Nazareth; the rider on the red horse, war, as red symbolizes blood; the rider on the black horse, famine; and on the pale green horse, death.

Horses appear again in *Revelation,* Chapter 19, verses 11 to 12: "Then I saw Heaven opened, and there was a white horse! Its rider is called Faithful and True, and . . . he has a name inscribed that no one knows but himself" (444-445NT). Not only are interpretations of these passages widespread, but so are their depictions and range of media and approaches used.

Horse warfare contrasted with the humble agriculture ass is common in biblical language. The uses and absences of their images in iconography add to the "totality of the unimaginable mystery" (Mathews 194). With both their presence and notable absence in iconography, horses touch human hearts and souls and ignite spiritual inspiration.

## The Horse and the Ass

Versions of tales from the ancient Greek storyteller Aesop have emerged across the globe throughout the ages reflecting countless tellers' and listeners' persuasions. Many variants of the following tale first found in *Aesop's Fables* have been told over time in the storytelling tradition. This version is said to be favored by some Christian storytellers.

*The Horse and the Ass* tells of a horse strutting proudly down a glistening road. Suddenly encountering an ass burdened with bundles on its back, the pompous horse shouts out to the ass to move aside. The ass obediently moves to the side of the road, muttering to himself about his bleak downtrodden station in life as a beast of burden while the horse is able to strut around like a king.

Soon the two meet again. This time the horse, weak and half-blind from the ravages of war, meanders down the road. The ass with bundles on his back sees the horse and, painfully observing how feeble the horse has become, appreciates his own health and fortunate circumstances. Likewise with this tale, audiences are reminded to harbor gratitude and contentment within their hearts rather than covetousness, and to treat others with humility, respect, and kindness.

## Unicorns in Jewish and Christian Mythologies

Greatly loved by humans throughout time, the legendary unicorn, or mythical horse with a single- or uni-horn, frolics through Jewish and Christian folklore just as it has been known to do through many mythologies across the globe since antiquity. Commonly depicted as a white horse with a horn (although petal pink, sunshine yellow, light lilac, and powder blue ones have graced some tales), unicorns have been attributed with many magical qualities. They are thought to be able to cure ills and banish evils. Often seen grazing or gazing in the flower meadows of our imaginations, the unicorn is considered playful, compassionate, honest, and pure of heart. In many cultures, the unicorn is a symbol of good luck.

## Unicorns in Jewish Lore

Unicorns do not shy away from Jewish lore. As legends go, some claim the unicorn refuses to go on Noah's Arc which is why we do not find unicorns on the earth today. Some say they prance around while the arc is leaving shore. Some say Noah chooses the lion over the unicorn when given the choice. Some say the first known compassionate unicorn misses the boat when trying to help others hop aboard. Others say the unicorn swims alongside the arc for forty days and forty nights but never comes aboard, thereby becoming extinct after the Giant Flood.[7] But unicorns, being the magical creatures they are, do still appear in tales today, so who knows? The lovely legendary uni-horned horses seem to have longevity, as they continue to show up in present-day media just as they had in tapestries and artwork throughout the ages.

Also, the Old Testament references the unicorn, possibly as the result of translators carrying the term over from earlier mythologies about a one-horned horse-like creature they refer to as a unicorn. For example, the *Book of Numbers* 23:22 in the Old Testament states: "God who brought them out of Egypt has as it were the strength of a unicorn."[8] Imagine! The all-powerful awesome God's strength is being associated with that of the unicorn, an association that migrates into Christian lore.

In addition, some consider references in the Old Testament to animals with a single horn to mean unicorns. For example, the *Book of Daniel* 8:5 states: "the he-goat *had* a conspicuous horn between his eyes" (1128). Many modern translations, however, translate these references to mean a wild ox or dog rather than a unicorn. Some also consider the Hebrew term *re'em*, formerly translated as unicorn, to mean wild bull.

## Unicorns in Christian Lore

The unicorn's precise origin is a mystery but is perhaps linked to engagements with rhinos or wild bulls in Persia, India, Tibet, or China. The unicorn is described by the Greek writer Ctesias in around 398 B.C.E., and then is described again in the second century A.C.E. in a book about animals called the *Physiologus* that tells of a unicorn being tamed by a virgin, a story that is a key to understanding early Christian lore.

Dating back to late Gothic times, the story of the unicorn and the virgin is portrayed in a series of seven tapestries called "The Hunt of the Unicorn" now hanging in The Cloisters in New York. Medieval books called *bestiaries* include descriptions and illustrations of the story of the unicorn and the virgin. Soon, medieval art and literature begin portraying the story with a Christian interpretation in which the unicorn, being associated with strength, represents Christ; the virgin is his mother, Mary.

Many stories arise. According to the lore, the horn of a unicorn can make poisonous waters safe. Placing his horn in a poisoned stream, the unicorn can purify the water before he is captured.

One interpretation of the story is that the poisoned water represents sin, the magical healing powers of the unicorn's horn represents Christ's healing powers, and the unicorn's capture represents Christ's arrest, trial, and crucifixion. However, there are many stories and many ways to understand each according to what we bring to them and find in them.

Today, unicorns come to life in stories that inspire imaginations to soar. They dance in moonlit nights, prance in magical forests, and whinny with glee atop rainbows. Appearing in books, TV shows, and movies for the young and young-at-heart, they continue to comfort us with their gifts of magic, gentle playful ways, and faithful friendship.

## Horse and Human Bonds Are Deep

Through the horse tales and myths of many cultures, we can appreciate the myriad roles the horse plays in lifting the human spirit. Encountering magical stallions, mares, and unicorns throughout our mythologies, as brought forth in oral traditions, storybooks, iconography, and other art forms, gives us glimpses into the horse archetypes that have influenced our cultures and guided our lives. These help connect us with our own soaring spirit that is sometimes diminished in our frenzied and fractured world. Engaging the equine archetypes that gallop through ancient and present-day myths and lore helps connect us with our own true nature or our natural essence and potential that seeks to be exercised and realized.

## Notes

1 Pamela Macgregor-Morris, ed. *The Book of the Horse* (NY: Exeter, 1979), 45. Further references to this work appear parenthetically in this work.

2 Elwyn Hartley Edwards. *The Encyclopedia of the Horse: The Definitive Guide to the Horse: the Major Breeds of the World, Their History & Modern Use.* (London, New York, Stuttgart, Moscow: Dorling Kindersley, 1994), 64.

3 M. Olden Howey, *The Horse in Magic and Myth* (Mineola, NY: Dover, 2002), 869. Further references to this work appear parenthetically in this work.

4 Isaac Bashevis Singer and Margot Zemach, *Naftali the Storyteller and His Horse, Sus, and Other Stories* (NY: Farrar, Straus and Giroux, 1976), 3. Further references to this work appear parenthetically in this work.

5 Thomas F. Mathews, *The Clash of Gods: A Reinterpretation of Early Christian Art, Revised and Expanded Edition* (Princeton and Oxford: Princeton UP, 1993), 129-131. Further references to this work appear parenthetically in this work.

6 Coogan, Michael D. ed. *The New Oxford Annotated Bible, Third Edition with the Apocryphal/ Deuterocanonical Books: New Revised Standard Version* (Oxford UP, 2001), 429NT. Further references to this work appear parenthetically in this work.

7 Skye Alexander, *Unicorns, the Myths, Legends, and Lore* (Avon, MA: Adams Media, 2015), 22. Further references to this work appear parenthetically in this work.

8 *The Holy Scripture, Revised in Accordance with Jewish Tradition and Modern Biblical Scholarship* (NY: Hebrew Publishing Co., 1939), 232. Further references to this work appear parenthetically in this work.

# Chapter 7

# Native American Horse Tales

## Horse Myths

Horses have special meaning for Native Americans who love to tell stories about the days when their horses are plentiful (Sherman 9). In these stories, horses speak, dance, fly, or dash faster than the wind, often in the service of taking their riders to accomplish great deeds. This chapter presents the deep relationships Native Americans have with their horses and the tales that emerge as a result. Affection, friendship, and the deep bonds between people and their horses come into focus.

Native Americans possess immense knowledge about horses. To learn the best ways to approach the steeds, they watch horses relate to each other, for they believe that each species has its own language and mental and emotional life. Traditionally, they believe that animals are not simply peoples, "but families within that peoplehood. It [is] therefore possible to establish intimate relationships with specific . . . animals and gain the precise knowledge that they [possess] about the world."[1] Imitating horses and other animals is not an option for Native Americans but is an imperative as it speaks of the intimacy of organic life (60).

Native Americans have always marveled at the behaviors of nature. For them, stories about horses and other animals can only be told in particular places and seasons out of their respect for the species. The key to understanding Native American knowledge of the world is to appreciate their emphasis on the particular rather than on the general laws of how things work, and to remember their "willingness to remain humble in spite of one's great knowledge" (22).

They are interested in personal relationships with nature and for them, all relationships have moral content. Therefore, their relationship with animals and nature is never separated from other sacred knowledge about ultimate spiritual realities. Thus, Native Americans focus on the completion of relationships and on the effect of their actions, such that to kill a horse requires the payment of respects to the species. Native Americans attend to the ways in which horses perceive and think about the world and attempt to understand their emotional experiences. Their stories reflect their respect for the horses' specific qualities and powers that they come to know (21-24).

## American Pawnee Old Dun Horse Tale

Many Native American myths and tales reveal not only the dynamic and vehicular power and magic of the horse, but also the special relationships they share. The North American Pawnee have one such horse tale. "Lone Boy and the Old Dun Horse" (Sherman 10) tells of a time when the Pawnee wander freely over the plains. In the story, an orphan boy named Lone Boy is so poor that he does not even have a horse to ride when his tribe packs up and rides on from one place to another. As he is walking after the tribe one day, he hears a feeble whinny and hurries down into a small ravine where he finds an old dun horse. Though he is laughed at for bothering with such a sad animal, Lone Boy chooses to care for the old horse, and later when the chief promises his beautiful daughter's hand in marriage to the hero who brings him a certain spotted calf hide, the old horse speaks to Lone Boy. "Don't worry," comforts the horse.

Lone Boy gasps, "You—you *spoke!*"

"Don't be afraid of me either. Come cover me with this nice, cool mud. . .. Give me the strength of the earth," he beseeches.

When the boy fulfills the request, the old horse is strong enough to transport Lone Boy to the spotted calf that immediately falls to the boy's arrows. After the boy proves himself worthy by caring for the horse and giving meat to those in need, the dun horse bestows upon the boy a herd of shining horses. As a result, with his spotted calf hide and wealth of horses, Lone Boy becomes the true hero that can wed the chief's daughter. The boy and his bride live happily together with the old dun horse remaining their treasured friend all their lives. The simple story conveys the power of the horse as a symbol of transformation.

## Shoshoni "Sky Dogs"

The best horses, the Mustang of Barb, Arabian, and Andalusia blood that once inhabit North America, become extinct about ten-thousand years ago and remain absent from the area until the Spanish Conquistador Cortez reintroduces them. When Native Americans first behold them, their riders appear to them as godlike creatures.

When the Spanish come to the Great Plains in the sixteenth century in search of land to conquer and goods to sell, they bring horses with them, some of which escape and raise offspring in the new land. The horses' arrival transforms Native American life. The nomadic tribes that had been foot wanderers can suddenly ride to grazing lands to hunt for buffalo and dash into battle against neighboring tribes. They replace their portable shelters with tipis and even develop a horse medicine cult.

When Antonio de Espejo first rides into Hopi land in 1583, the Native Americans—having never before seen a horse—pave the grounds with ceremonial quilts for the sacred beasts to walk upon. By the end of the seventeenth century, Wyoming Shoshonis obtain horses from Colorado Utes. The rapid spread of horses throughout the Plains gives rise to a new Native American way of life characterized around the world by the Appaloosa-riding, war-bonneted warrior.[2]

Great Plains people become adept at riding horses. They often ride bareback, using a single leather band as a bridle. For them, horses rapidly become the source of transport, warfare, and mobility. Further, horses become the symbols of wealth. The more they own, the greater their status in the tribe.[3] Widely used as a medium of exchange, men give horses to women's families as dowries. Stealing horses from neighboring tribes become acts of bravery. Referred to as 'sky dogs' by people of the far western plains, horses inspire a cultural revolution (Nabokov 42). Trading and raiding times shorten, and mounted tribes, like the Shoshoni, become lords of the northern plains.

## The Girl Who Loved Wild Horses

With horses to ride on their hunt and transport their belongings, a Native American tribe packs up to leave and follow the buffalo. In the village where they stop is a Native American girl who loves wild horses. They watch her as she leads the wild horses to drink at the river and then as she naps with them in the meadow, speaks to them, and treats their wounds. They see that she understands horses in a special way.

One sunny day while the wild horses are eating amidst the flowers, she falls asleep. Suddenly, either in her dream's eye or waking life, she leaps up as thunder and lightning descend upon her and the wild horses in a huge frightful storm. She jumps onto a horse and forcefully rides with the band of wild horses to safety. Soon the storm ends, and a handsome stallion welcomes her to come and live with the wild horses.

Time passes and the villagers miss the girl who loves wild horses. After searching for her, they bring her home to live with her parents. But the girl misses the wild horses. Only after she becomes incurably ill do her parents understand her yearning to return to the wild horses and, because they love her, let her go. Once again free to live with the wild horses, she does not forget her people and returns each year to bring her parents a colt. When she does not return, a group goes out to find her. Instead of finding her with the horses, they find the stallion she favors standing with a beautiful mare. The girl who loves wild horses has become one of the wild horses she loves.

Inspiring heartbeats with every hoof beat, Paul Goble's book *The Girl Who Loved Wild Horses* [4] tugs at the heartstrings of the young and young-at-heart who love horses or dreams of horses. This heartwarming tale of a girl who understands and loves horses, ultimately becoming one, reflects the ways in which Native Americans honor, respect, and revere horses. With horses transforming their lives forever, changing them from a nomadic to a riding people able to hunt and trade, the horses have become symbols of freedom for them, as this tender tale reveals.

## Blackfoot Tribe's "Many Horses"

In the early nineteenth century, Wolf Calf, a Piegan, or member of the southernmost Blackfoot tribe, tells a story to the Plains Indian scholar George Bird Grinnell of the tribes' first sight of horses and of a chief whose name changes from "Dog" to "Many Horses".

The story begins with a band of Piegans who camp at a spot where they jump buffalo and are having a great day, with much meat to eat. A Kutenai, their enemy, is buffalo hunting on horseback and is having a bad day. Rather than starve his family, the Kutenai rides over to the nearby Piegans to ask for meat. Upon seeing the horse, the Piegans are bewildered and afraid. As it comes closer, they can see that it is a man on some sort of animal and ask their chief to go forward and talk to him.

Hesitantly, the chief approaches the Kutenai and together they agree to exchange a horse for a meal for his family. Soon they become friends and the Kutanai brings over all of his horses, becomes head chief of the Piegans, and changes his name from "Dog" to "Sits-in-the Middle" to "Many Horses". He and the tribe that becomes his people have enough horses to trade some for fine things, including their first guns from white men (Nabakov 42-44).

Such stories change with each teller and telling and are enjoyable for the meanings that audiences both bring to them and find in them. For some, this is a tale that speaks of the horse as an agent of cultural change. While its meanings are specific to the Native American experience, the images represented reveal patterns that exist in the collective psyche.

## A Geronimo Story

A tale comes to life in Leslie Marmon Silko's *Storyteller* demonstrating the fondness and friendship between the Navajos and their horses. "A Geronimo Story" opens with scouts in a corral saddling up so they can hunt for Geronimo. As they do, their horses bolt and try to back away. The storyteller's and her Uncle Siteye's horses are missing so she concludes they are not going to help track Geronimo. But her uncle assures her that they are going. She then finds and saddles up her uncle's tall strong horse Rainbow, as it sighs "like horses do when you cinch them up good and they know you've got them" and her old-time

Indian horse, "the kind . . . that can run all day, and they don't get tired."[5]

They enjoy the beauty of the journey, feeding and caring for the horses that take them up the mountains and across the canyons, rocks, and streams. Masquerading as hunters in search of Geronimo, they covertly steer the enemy away to protect him. When the storyteller comments to her Uncle Siteye, "[Geronimo] always gets away," he stares up at the stars and replies, "but I always like to think that it's us who get away" (222).

In this lovely tale, Silko expresses the plight of her people as she describes an uncle in the cunning act of misleading Geronimo's hunters in order to protect Geronimo and, in effect, himself and their people. The horses are their friends, each horse knowing its rider so very well.

## Ghost Dance at Wounded Knee

George Eagle Elk at Parmelee, Rosebud Indian Reservation in South Dakota shares a Brule Sioux story, "Tatanka Iyotake's Dancing Horse," as recorded by Richard Erdoes and Alfonso Ortiz. The tale is of a magical white horse that dances and prances to honor its dead master "in the only way it knew," though onlookers think it is possessed "in the spirit way." It begins with a ghost dance at Wounded Knee.[6]

Now, for those with a clear conscience, a ghost dance can be peaceful, but for the white people who had "taken away half of the remaining Indian land just a few years before" (267), it is not peaceful, for they bring to it a bad conscious and their own fears. At the time, Sitting Bull, or Tatanka Iyotake as he is called in Sioux, is the holy man and spiritual leader of the Sioux nation, and he always said, "I want the white man beside me, not above me" (267).

Tatanka Iyotake befriends Buffalo Bill Cody who gives him his favorite white circus horse that can perform many tricks. At the same time, Tatanka Iyotake opposes, and becomes the enemy of, those who want Native Americans to lose their identity to the ways of the whites.

The ghost dance becomes the occasion to get rid of Tatanka Iyotake who is accused of protecting the ghost dancers and standing in the way of progress for those who want the Native Americans "to die out" (268).

He is shot to death by Native American warriors in police garb. The shooting triggers his white horse to perform circus tricks, as it had done routinely in Buffalo Bill Cody's Wild West Show. The horse dances and prances late into the night after the fight is over. Thus, Tatanka Iyotake and the white horse live on as a legend of its people (267-269).

This legend changes in the retelling as legends always do. Revealing the inhumane treatment of Native Americans by American officials, it shows the loyalty of the horse that symbolizes the dancing god and life eternal. While there are many ways to understand legends, Erdoes and Ortiz suggest, "They are emblems of a living religion, giving concrete form to a set of beliefs and traditions that link people living today to ancestors from centuries and millennia past" (xv).

## Joseph Campbell and Buffalo Bill Cody

Mythologist Joseph Campbell is introduced to the Native Americans when Buffalo Bill Cody brings the Wild West Show to Madison Square Garden. His interest grows as he reads their myths and digs for their arrowheads in the backyards of Delaware (Campbell, *Power* 10). He comes to understand that the people of the Great Plains do not regard animals as subspecies, but rather as their equals and, in some instances, their superiors. They recognize that animals have some powers humans do not. That is why a shaman, for example, often has the spirit of an animal close by as a teacher and an adviser on how to live (75).

Campbell explains a Pawnee's belief as follows. In the beginning of all things, wisdom and knowledge are with the animals, and the One Above sends certain animals to let humans know he shows himself not only through the sun, moon, and stars, but through animals from whom humans need to learn. With this, Campbell senses a stirring in the mythic imagination, the wonder of things (79).

Campbell observes that when the Native Americans receive horses from the Spaniards, they are then able to venture out of the plains and take part in the great hunt. He sees their mythology transform from vegetarian to buffalo and from this learns that people respond to their environment. For him, this shows myth is alive and able to inspire people to mythologize their environment and world (85).

## Black Elk's Story

Joseph Campbell speaks of Black Elk's account of a sick boy who spiritually rises from a teepee to a landscape of clouds where he receives a visit from a bay horse. The bay speaks to him of its history that he wants the boy to see, as follows: "Westward stand twelve black horses; Northward, twelve white ones; Eastward, twelve sorrel horses; and Southward, twelve buckskins," he recounts. "Forty-eight horses stand firmly in formation behind the bay," he continues. A "Storm of plunging horses in all colors that shake the world, neighing back. 'See,' said the bay, 'how your horses all come dancing!' And there were horses everywhere, a skyfull, dancing, that changed into all kinds of animals and vanished to the quarters."[7]

Adventures ensue as the bay, with the procession of fine horses behind him, carries the boy through a series of ascents. As Campbell affirms, "the high roles of . . . the horse . . . are of the architecture of the mythic world of the North American plains heritage" (91). The colorful dancing horses are a vision, universal in its archetypal nature and personal as it reflects the youth's locality and North American plains' heritage. As symbols of transformation, they bring hope and comfort.

## Oglala Sioux's Crazy Horse Story

Within the Native American mythologies is a story of the great Oglala Sioux leader who bears the name of the powerful steed, Crazy Horse. As a youth, he loves horses and is given a pony by his father. The youth becomes a fine horseman. A gentle warrior and a true brave, Crazy Horse stands for the highest ideals of the Sioux. With a big heart and personal commitment to public service, he earns recognition as a visionary leader who is determined to help preserve the traditions and values of the Lakota people.

Crazy Horse believes that soldiers had been sent to destroy their reservations. When General Custer, or Long Hair as they call him, comes to fight, the Sioux want to leave with their squaws but know they must defend themselves. Therefore, they massacre Custer's troops.

Afterward, Crazy Horse attempts to live in peace in Canada, but the American government pursues him. He returns to the Red Cloud

Agency to discuss ways to achieve peace. He is killed. When bayoneted by a Sioux guard at Fort Robinson, Nebraska in 1877, his final words are thought to be these: "My friend, I do not blame you for this. . . . At times we did not get enough to eat, and we were not allowed to leave the reservation to hunt. . . . We preferred our own way of living. We were no expense to the government then. All we wanted was peace and to be left alone" (Nabokov 178-179). He ends his final speech with the memorable words: "I have spoken."

His vision and deeds live on in the hearts of his people and of those who read and hear about his life and story. To honor Crazy Horse's life and legacy that includes his vision of a better future for not only his people but everyone, the Oglala Lakota leader, Chief Henry Standing Bear ("Mato Naji"), a prominent statesman and elder in the Native American community, recruits and commissions Polish-American sculptor Korczak Ziolkowski to build the Crazy Horse Memorial in the Black Hills of South Dakota roughly seventeen miles from Mount Rushmore, a major undertaking that breaks ground in 1948. This tribute to the Lakota leader Crazy Horse not only is to be the largest mountain carving in South Dakota and the world but, with an on-site Indian Museum of the North American and Native American Educational and Cultural Center, is to be a remarkable tribute that attracts visitors from every corner of the earth, inspires imaginations, and keeps the ideas to which Crazy Horse is committed alive.

## Horses Lift the Human Spirit

As long as horses continue to charge forth, carrying riders into streams, onto mountaintops, along pathways, and through passages, they will continue to inspire the mythic imagination. The image gives rise to tales of old dun horses that can speak and transform lives, and white circus horses that dance to honor their masters and carry the human spirit forward. The horse also bears witness to the need to respect and protect the Geronimos and Crazy Horses of the world, whose plights are a painful part of our human history.

As horses harness themselves to the winds and dash forward with their manes  and tales flying, they warm and delight the human heart and ignite the imagination. Through the legends, myths, and tales of the Native Americans and other cultures, we can appreciate the myriad roles that the horse plays in lifting the human spirit. Tending to horses as the Native Americans do, watching them relate to one another, and getting to know their particular ways, allows us to gain enhanced perspectives for understanding animals, nature, and our own place and meaning in the world.

## Notes

1 Vine Deloria, Jr. and Daniel R. Wildcat, *Power and Place: Indian Education in America* (Golden, Colorado: Fulcrum Resources, 2001), 59. Further references to this work appear parenthetically in this work.

2 Peter Nabokov, ed. *Native American Testimony: A Chronicle of Eastern-White Relations from Prophecy to the Present, 1492-2000, rev Edition* (NY: Penguin, 1999), 35. Further references to this work appear parenthetically in this work.

3 Tim McNeese, ed. *Myths of Native America* (NY: Four Walls Eight Windows, 1999), 128-129. Further references to this work appear parenthetically in this work.

4 Paul Goble, *The Girl Who Loved Wild Horses* (NY: Aladdin, 1978). Further references to this work appear parenthetically in this work.

5 Leslie Marmon Silko, *Storyteller* (NY: Arcade, 1981), 213. Further references to this work appear parenthetically in this work.

6 Richard Erdoes and Alfonso Ortiz, eds, *American Indian Myths and Legends* (NY: Pantheon, 1984), 269. Further references to this work appear parenthetically in this work.

7 Joseph Campbell, *The Flight of the Wild Gander: Explorations in the Mythological Dimension (Selected Essays 1944-1968)*, (Novato, California: New World Library, 2002), 88-89. Further references to this work appear parenthetically in this work.

Chapter 8

# Saddling Up with Horse Tales

## Human-Horse Team

Ever since humans first teamed up with horses, humans have carried forth inspirational stories about the magnificent creatures. These stories as conveyed through the literary and fine arts from generation to generation across cultures throughout the globe are rich and profound. These are the hoof prints in the sand reminding us how deeply horses have contributed to human lives and permeate the human psyche.

In many parts of the world, newspapers, radios, magazine and online event calendars, and Facebook postings are filled with opportunities to team up with horses and enjoy pleasure-riding on horseback or in horse-drawn carriages; participate in trail riding, jousting, jumping, and other equestrian sports; and attend or take part in horse shows, polo matches, roping games, and rodeo events. Books, paintings, and sculptures bring symbolic, mythological, and natural horses into our homes and hearts. For the fortunate who have neighborhood libraries, libraries on wheels, and bookstores; for the many who have access to books online (for purchase or instant download) and books on tape; and for those who are able to visit museums and galleries both virtual and real, a variety of portrayals, interpretations, and renditions of horses and horse tales are available.

## Horses in Books Abound

Such popular books as Jonathan Swift's *Gulliver's Travels* (1726), Anna Sewell's *Black Beauty* (1877) with its multiple film adaptations; John Steinbeck's *The Red Pony* (1933) later made into a movie by the same name (1949); Enid Algerine Bagnold's *National Velvet* (1935) with its movie adaption starring Elizabeth Taylor and Mickey Rooney (1944); Walter Lorimer Farley's *The Black Stallion* (1941) with its many sequels and a television series (1990-1993); Mildred Mastin Pace's *Old Bones the Wonder Horse* (1955); Marguerite Henry's *King of the Wind: The Story of the Godolphin Arabian* (1990); Cormac McCarthy's *All the Pretty Horses* (1993); Pam Munoz Ryan's *Paint the Wind* (2007); Bonnie Bryant's *Saddle Club Series* (1988-2001) and TV series (2001), are among the many books with which we all saddle up on our couches, under cozy blankets, to read while sipping hot cocoa. An example follows.

## Horses in Jonathan Swift's Gulliver's Travels

The talking horses that band together in the remarkable misadventures of Jonathon Swift's *Gulliver's Travels* (1726) are unforgettable.[1] The protagonist, world traveler Lemuel Gulliver, stumbles upon them in Part IV of a book long considered a classic of English literature and thank goodness. The humans called *Yahoos* in Part IV are despicable, leaving Gulliver without any options other than to join the household of horses he comes to admire.

In *Part IV: A Voyage to the Country of the Houyhnhnms*, the latter being the name of the race of talking horses who rule the land, Gulliver discovers that unlike the humans he has come to know, horses are able to live together in peace—without mistreating each other with violence and petty emotions. In fact, they do not exhibit emotions, only reason. Furthermore, they do not express opinions—or individuality, for that matter. The Houyhnhnms value the exchange of ideas without having to convince others of their views and, above all, they value friendship.

In the end, after being rejected by the horses for being human, Gulliver manages to paddle off in a canoe and catch a ride on a ship until he eventually makes his way home, but not without leaving his heart in the land of the Houyhnhnms, wishing he could one day leave the humans and return to live among the horses. In the meantime, he buys two young stallions that he keeps in a stable and speaks with daily to keep himself from going mad.

Like all myths, there are many ways to understand Gulliver and the horses. Among these is an appreciation for the grandeur of the horse which Jonathan Swift selects to use, perhaps, as a mirror to see humans from outsider perspectives. Even so, the remarkable misadventures that come to life in *Gulliver's Travels* cast a light on the good nature of horses, even if inadvertently.

## Horses in Poetry

Vast arrays of poetry centered on horses warm audiences' hearts. Some celebrate special relationships and magical secrets cherished between children and their steeds. One such poem is of a fly-away horse taking a child to magical places at night, places a grandma might not believe are real. Eugene Field's poem "The Fly-Away Horse" (mid-1800s) is such a poem: "And the Fly Away Horse seeks those faraway lands" about which children dream at night, lands filled with candy trees, honey brooks, white-popcorn fields, beasts who are good, and monkeys who play. Riding a fly-away horse, anyone's dreams might soar.

Poetry centered on horses also herald in the longing for the smells, tastes, and grit of days long gone. As Edwin Muir's poem "The Horses" (1956) reminds us: "We had sold our horses in our fathers' time" and now children no longer, we have bought and use new tractors to pull our ploughs once pulled by our fabulous steeds, a change that brings with it our new lives.

Also, poems of human and horse companionship, endurance, symbolic passages, and more, touch our hearts. From Rudyard Kipling's poem "White Horses" (1897) to Carl Sandburg's poems "Bronzes" (1916) and "Horses and Men in Rain" (1918), to D. H. (David Herbert) Lawrence's poem "The White Horse" (1964), equestrian-centered and themed poems take us away to a world (or Otherworld) horse lovers will never forget. An example follows.

## Sylvia Plath's "Ariel"—A Horse Race

As universal symbols of the imagination, horses may serve as passages to other realms. Such symbols recall mythological journeys, such as that of the ancient Egyptian Sun god who sails through the night-sea, or world of the deceased, only to be challenged by monsters that must be overcome for the sun to rise each morning rejuvenated. As if riding the horse through a symbolic passage, Sylvia Plath's postmodern poem "Ariel," published in 1965[2] after the poet's death, transports its readers and listeners through a night-sea journey into the morning sun. With imagery that evokes a return to the realm of the spirit in its struggle against nature, awakening consciousness to the oblivion of existence and to eternity, the poem feverishly yet eerily drives toward a radiant spiritual light employing the forceful gait of a racehorse.

Starting with "Stasis in darkness," the poem evokes the inactivity that results from the pulls of opposing forces, like a restrained horse that is ready to charge, yet in darkness. *Darkness* in myths often points to the underworld, or to the plight of humans who operate without an awareness of the forces that shape their lives.

With the words "Then the substance less blue," there is life. One can almost see the horse, once restrained, now dash so forcefully that it does not leave a trace in the blue sky. "Pour of tor and distances" furthers the horse metaphor. The meter of the measured syllables in "Pour of tor," when repeated aloud, mimics the thunderous beat of hoofs pounding into the earth. *Tor* points to the hard downpour of torrential rains, like hoofs' repetitive pounding as the horse charges forth toward the finish line.

The lines "How one we grow, / Pivot of heels and knees!" point to the act of merging and suggest a union of horse and rider, a joining together in wholeness. Here the imagery moves with a "Pivot of heels and knees!" with *pivot* being that point on which things turn; *heels* being our bodies' foundations that, if affected, cause the body to fall; and *knees* being our power, for to bring someone to their knees is to impose will upon them (Chevalier and Gheerbrant 490, 573). These images evoke a journey forward from death or darkness into life, as when the horse and jockey, perhaps once falling behind, now round the mark to achieve their goal of winning.

The journey moves ahead with the lightning speed of a triple-crown sweep. In "White / Godiva, I unpeel— / Dead hands," *white* symbolizes illumination, transcendent perfection, purity, or triumph of the spirit over flesh; it represents death, rebirth, and surrender (Cooper 4142). *Godiva* is a legendary goddess who rides naked on a horse through the streets. *Hands* are creative life-giving powers (78). In the spirit of Godiva, earthly garments are shed, and hands as creative powers die. With fewer encumbrances, one can imagine the omniscient narrator shooting off like a rocket, a fertile arrow, or a sizzling horse racing down the track toward the shiny medal of victory.

The poem concludes: "And now I / Am the arrow." Notably, it states not, "I am *like* the arrow" but rather "I am the arrow." Here, the poem's voice is that of the arrow calling forth the image of a darting projectile, a missile, or a horse charging down the track. Throughout "Ariel," images race from a state of immobility, rich in its mythic meanings of death and the underworld, through life, toward rebirth or new beginnings. The images represent opposites in a single portrayal of death and life, or night's darkness and the cauldron of morning. Within Sylvia Plath's poem "Ariel" is an exquisite mythological horse race between earthly and spiritual realms.

## Horses in the Visual Arts

Horses in swift movement have been widely displayed since prehistoric times, first as paintings on cave walls. According to Christopher Brown, "The wild, springing creatures drawn on the cave walls at Lascaux, France are probably a prayer of our ancestors of 20,000 years ago that the swift horse might stay in range of their spears; by painting a picture of the animal, they capture the spirit of it and so gain ascendancy over it."[3] Such early representations communicate the likely presence and spiritual significance of horses in the area. Throughout the ages, the horse has been a favorite subject for artists, and its images continue to exercise their "magic still" (51).

Artwork depicting horses, from the paintings found on the prehistoric Lascaux cave walls to the ancient Uffington White Horse of the Iron- or late Bronze-Age looking much like a white chalk-etched figure on an English hillside called White Horse Hill, also document our human and horse history. These show the prominence the ancients placed on horse images. Paintings and pottery from ancient Egypt and Greece honor the equine image. The Renaissance period in Europe, with such artists as Leonardo da Vinci and Raphael, depicts the horse in brilliant colors. In the Baroque period, with artists such as Peter Paul Rubens, Anthony van Dyck, and Diego Velazquez, horses in paintings charge forth with billowing manes and wild movement.

In the mid-eighteenth-century Romantic period in art, such renowned French artists as Eugene Delacroix bring horses to life in their works. In 1724, George Stubbs paints so many horse images that he becomes known as "the horse painter". In nineteenth-century France with horse racing rising in popularity, the horse stories continue with artists such as the Impressionist Edgar Degas painting stunning horse portrayals. In the twentieth century, such notables as Wassily Kandinsky paints abstract horses with riders, as in his 1911 painting referred to as "Man on a Horse," and pop art master Andy Warhol creates a silk screen image of the four-time Kentucky Derby-winning jockey Bill Shoemaker in 1978, focusing on the glamor of horse racing. Also in the twentieth century, Pablo Picasso, Henri Matisse, and Marc Chagall are among the many artists who bring horses to life in their own ways. Twentieth-first century artists continue to inspire our imaginations with equestrian imagery in a variety of media, connecting with our memories, dreams, and experiences associated with horses.

A few examples of artists bringing horses to life in their artwork follow. Some portray horses carrying goddesses and knights. Others present them as representations of the natural world in contrast with artificiality. Some feature horses as mythological symbols of life fighting against the boundaries of death. In these and so many other works of art, horses spring to life tapping into the depths of our psyches, releasing our energy, igniting our imaginations, touching our hearts, and inspiring our souls.

## George Stubbs's "Whistlejacket"

To see what a horse actually looks like, from his skeletal structure to his musculature, and how the horse behaves in a variety of situations, from performing among other horses and humans at the racetrack to mingling and fighting with other animals in the wild, audiences need look no further than George Stubbs's paintings and prints. George Stubbs, who lives from 1724 to 1806, is an English painter widely known as "the horse painter" whose studies and artistic renditions of horses are as romantic as the portraits done of humans, so popular during his time.

Stubbs brings to life the powerful and highly celebrated horse Whistlejacket, standing alone against a plain background except for a few shadows beneath the horse's hind legs, in his painting of the same name now located in the National Gallery in London. The life-sized portrait of the grand horse is as dramatic as it is inspiring, as the horse's beauty as portrayed is awesome. Having started his horse-painting career by dissecting and studying horses, no one is better prepared to bring the majestic animal into the art world and beyond than Stubbs.

Privately commissioned to paint portraits of horse owners' and breeders' favorite horses, he captures the equine excitement in his pictures of racehorses, carriage horses, and farm horses with brilliance and precision. Further, he brings horses' behaviors to life in vivid color. Showing horses in service to humans in civilized environments, interacting with each other in fields, farms, cliffs, and rocky ridges, and fighting wildly with lions, his paintings reveal the horses' many temperaments amidst not only the serene but the savage sides of nature, inspiring viewers to tangle with horses in their waking life's imaginations and nighttime's dreams.

## Rosa Bonheur's "The Horse Fair"

The strikingly handsome white, black, brown, and dappled grey horses depicted in the painting "The Horse Fair" that appear to be indefatigably circling round the field, some with riders, some being pulled by ropes, are captivating and energizing. The horses seem to be alive. With the action so immediate and the scene so realistic, the painting's viewers almost feel compelled to go home and change into dirty trousers before continuing their involvement in the work of art.

Deserving of much attention is the remarkable painter of "The Horse Fair," Rosa Bonheur, who lives from 1822 to 1899 in France. Creator of the eight-foot by sixteen-foot masterpiece, she often dresses like a man so she can sketch and paint unobtrusively. The cigar-smoking short-haired woman in men's clothing clandestinely sneaks into many environments traditionally visited only by men in order to study the animals she loves. The painting "The Horse Fair" reflects her intense study of horses at the horse fairs she frequents in men's garb, where women are not normally permitted.

Her paintings are realistic, showing horses as horses and men as men all negotiating for power in an equal playing field. Influenced by her socialist parents, she paints subjects traditionally painted by men thereby setting examples for other aspiring women artists.[4]

## John Maler Collier's "Lady Godiva"

A painter in the Pre-Raphaelite style, John Maler Collier, a prominent British writer and painter living from 1850 to 1934, is known for painting classical subjects in a dramatic theatrical style. A true romantic, he delights in illustrating scenes from myths, legends, and literature, often with a focus on beautiful women. His painting "Lady Godiva" brings to life a stunning legendary Lady who is conscious of her nudity as she, according to her myths, rides for a cause through the city streets on a white horse.

Myths dating back to the thirteenth century tell her story as follows. Lady Godiva is an eleventh-century Anglo-Saxon noblewoman who rides naked on a white horse through the streets of Coventry, covered only by her long hair, in exchange for her husband's agreeing to lower his tenants' oppressive taxes. In Collier's painting that furthers the myth, her head is lowered, and her eyes are cast downward. Remarkable for her beauty and suffering, Godiva's introversion as portrayed in the painting evokes an atmosphere associated with tortured beings who struggle with conflicted emotions over their tangled actions and circumstances. Perhaps she is unsure that her husband will honor his agreement or that the city's inhabitants will refrain from glancing at her as asked. Collier's portrayal of her with her head held down in contrast with the horse's head held high gives the myth depth; the Lady, mysteriousness; and the painting, an allure.

That Collier depicts Lady Godiva seated on a white horse is significant. Riding the decorated white horse, with *white horse* being an "image of beauty gained when the spirit . . . controls the senses, [an image that conjures] the process of ascension, [as] all great Messianic figures ride such horses" (Chevalier and Gheerbrant 525), Lady Godiva is given the stature of a deity, as deities throughout the mythologies of many lands ride white horses. Linking her with deities such as Epona in Celtic myths and Rhiannon, her equivalent in Welsh myths, Collier's painting captures Lady Godiva's magic and magnificence. Seated on the majestic white horse, which is widely associated in mythology with purity, spirituality, and ascension, this romantic image of the notoriously beautiful Lady Godiva is brilliant and inspiring.

## William Morris's "The Arming and Departure of the Knights"

Magnificent horses carrying knights in armor during jousts, pageantry, and battles have been depicted in the arts for thousands of years. The medieval armored knight on horseback, revered as a figure of romance, is widely portrayed in the visual arts in various media, including ceramic tile, terracotta reliefs, and paintings on parchment, coins, and more.

A lover of nature, fairies, and knights, William Morris, a British writer, artist, and socialist who lives from 1834 to 1896, revives art forms and subject matter from the Middle Ages, hoping to recapture the heroism, romance, and authenticity of the earlier age. Capturing the spirit of wonder, he portrays scenes of heroes and romances from legends. He brings to life a time when the natural and supernatural are all one in the medieval world that does not divide them.[5] His tapestries, stained glass, poetry, and other forms of artistic expression weave together gods, goddesses, angels, fairies, and horses, revealing the wonder of their stories and adventures.

While art is flourishing in nineteenth-century England, Morris believes the authenticity of handicrafts is being lost in mass production and is committed to resurrecting lost techniques for printing and the making of stained glass and tapestries. Along with Edward Burne-Jones and others in the Pre-Raphaelite movement who turn to medieval art for inspiration, Morris revives medieval tapestry production methods and designs. He builds the traditional high-warp loom, teaches himself how to weave, and founds a textile production company, Morris, Marshall, Faulkner & Company in 1861, later called Morris and Company. Morris and Edward Burne-Jones both create many tapestries of medieval scenes with knights riding their decorated horses on quests and in battle.

Inspired by Sir Thomas Malory's *Le Morte D'Arthur*,[6] the tapestry called "The Arming and Departure of the Knights," which Morris produces in the 1890s, is one of six woven panels portraying the Holy Grail Quest. This panel shows Sir Lancelot on horseback ready to depart, with Lady Guinevere handing him a shield. The tapestry is one of many that show the intrinsic role of gallant horses in the execution of knights' duties. "The Knights" tapestry woven by Morris & Company in 1890 is another showing riders mounted on noble steeds at the knights' departure.

## Franz Marc's "Blue Horses"

In the symbolic painting entitled "Blue Horses" or "The Large Blue Horses," equine images roll like the hillsides behind them, all gracefully informing viewers of the rhythms and harmony in nature. "Blue Horses" is one among many of Franz Marc's paintings in which he portrays horses in blue. The color blue for Marc represents the spirit. For him, horses are transcendental; they represent the capacity to transcend the material world.

In other paintings, Marc depicts horses in reds and yellows, each carrying particular emotional tones and attitudes. A painter and printmaker in the German Expressionist movement and a founder of

The Blue Rider group of artists that turn away from nature and past traditions for inspiration, turning instead to the emotions reality evokes, Franz Marc lives from 1880 to 1916, only thirty-six years.[7] Born in Germany and spending some years in France, Marc favors using animals as the subject of his artwork, as he finds them to be pure in spirit, and translucent colors to express feelings about animals and the constricting world in which they live.

## Pablo Picasso's "Guernica"

Being highly symbolic, horses are painted by many of the world's greatest artists, including Pablo Picasso who, born in Spain, lives from 1881 to 1973 producing twenty thousand pieces of art during his career, with his 1937 Cubist painting "Guernica" being among the most well-known. Notably in Picasso's "Guernica" a wounded horse is the central image likely representing the people and animals brutally victimized, wounded, and slaughtered from the ravages of war. With a lightbulb above the horse's head and a candle nearby, both casting beams of light onto the horse, the horse is clearly the painting's focal point. With its newsprint coat, the horse may be the symbolic messenger or news vehicle, speaking out on behalf of saving the vulnerable people and animals of this world, and specifically the village of Guernica, from being wounded or destroyed.

With images that are ambiguous and open to wide interpretation, the painting is likely portraying the suffering that wars inflict upon innocent people and animals, with the horse symbolizing the people of Guernica, in opposition to the bull in the painting that likely represents both the onslaught of fascism as well as Spain where bullfighting is popular.

Picasso's painting is widely appreciated as an antiwar response to the Nazis' bombing of Guernica, a Basque town near his homeland, Spain, during the Spanish Civil War. With the painting being so busy, having images of animals and people all jumbled together, it may evoke within its audiences the feeling of being immersed in Guernica and unable to escape the horrors of war, just as the citizens of Guernica are unable to escape.

In his book *The Masks of God: Creative Mythology*, Joseph Campbell sheds light on Picasso's "Guernica" imparting that within the painting, "a horse and its rider lie shattered, and a bull stands mighty and whole." Campbell references two significant transformative events in human mobility: the first, the change from humans walking to their riding horses and horse-drawn chariots; the second, the displacement of humans riding their horses using horsepower (209-210). He interprets the wounded horse and other figures in the painting as representations of the end of the old order of power and, in contrast, the shining electric light bulb as a representation of the new order of power. Rather than search for the symbolic figures' final meaning, he suggests that mythic symbols, like Picasso's wounded horse, have many meanings; furthermore, their symbolism points beyond meaning. To give them a final meaning would be to extract the life out of them. The use of mythological symbols in art connects viewers with images from their own dreams and waking life, as these images are rooted in history and the archetypes of the psyche. Left ambiguous, they are inspiring, stimulating, and energizing (671-672).

Pablo Picasso's infamous "Guernica" is among his many paintings that feature equine images in a variety of settings and circumstances, revealing his passion for horses. Ever since painting "Boy Leading a Horse" at the age of eight in Malaga, Picasso paints numerous pictures of horses that he finds to be fabulous and fantastic. From "The Horsehead" to the "Bullfight" and "Horse with a Youth in Blue," Picasso's work shows the horse to be mythical, magical, and magnificent. Portraying all types of horses, from the highly symbolic white-winged Pegasus to the circus horse and stud steed, Picasso's paintings, drawings, and engravings bring horses, with their wide-ranging attributes, to life.

## Henri Matisse's "The Horse, the Rider and the Clown"

Gracefully bowing his violet-colored head, the horse in Matisse's "The Horse, the Rider and the Clown" is vibrant and full of life. This horse, produced in 1943 by Henri Emile Benoit Matisse who lives from 1869 to 1954, may reflect the artist's upbringing in a small French town in which people continue to ride on horseback, for horses are the subjects in many of his works. Other examples of Matisse's horse-centered works include a 1904 painting entitled "Pierre with Wooden Horse" depicting a young boy in red garb affectionately holding a white and black wooden horse in his arms just as a mom would cuddle her precious baby, and a 1937 colored offset lithograph entitled "Horse and Wagon" depicting a white horse silhouette on a black background within a highly-decorated rose, white, and yellow frame.

More than his childhood memories, the horse in "The Horse, the Rider and the Clown" represents a circus horse, reflecting the circus-themed book for which it is intended. The artwork is done as a Cut-Out for Matisse's 1947 illustrated book, *Jazz*, in a style he adopts using a scissors for cutting shapes out of paper  to express his imagery in paper much the way he uses a paintbrush earlier in his career. The highly decorated wallpaper-like background is exuberant, evoking the sounds of jugglers, musicians, dancers, and other circus performers; the movements of trained animals and spirited crowds; and the smells of corn, candy, and drinks of all kinds. The vivid artwork is so engaging, viewers likely experience the excitement of the circus being in town.

Matisse brings to life a horse that is bold and energetic. Appreciated for his distinctive rhythm of line, harmony of color, and commitment to bringing the emotional sense of objects to life, Matisse creates a horse that evokes in his viewers the thrill of mounting and forcefully riding. After he is diagnosed with cancer and confined to a wheelchair, he cuts the colorful shapes and patterns with the passion of someone who is in a race against time, or a horse race that he is determined to win.

## Marc Chagall's "Peasant Life"

Marc Zakharovich Chagall, the Russian-born modernist artist who lives from 1887 to 1985, spends many of his formative years in Paris. Throughout his career, he works in paint, stained glass, tapestry, mosaics, sculpture, and other media in portraying perceptions of dreams, visions, and legends with a deep understanding of Jewish mysticism from his heritage and the ability to transform emotions into great works of art. His work is riddled with visionary images projected with a hallucinatory quality using deeply intense luscious colors. Several of his masterpieces feature a horse.

Painted in 1925, "Peasant Life" shows a large horse in white, yellow, and blue with a patch of green, being fed by a peasant boy in a bright-red Russian cap and dark-blue jacket.

Against the colorful peasant, the horse looks pale, almost ethereal, and definitely dreamlike. On the arc of the horse's neck, a couple in peasant garb appears to be dancing in the distance while a green horse, harkening back to the green patch on the larger central horse, is pulling a coach in which sit a driver and a gentleman. With the little lopsided red house to the left of the horse and parallel with the arc of his neck, the picture appears to be portraying a Russian village through the eyes of a French romantic, done with the artistry of a skilled colorist. The beautiful ethereal horse could either be the dreamer or the dream.

Painted in 1927, "Equestrienne" emerges from, and reflects, Chagall's love of the circus with its fantasy, flair, and artificiality. With an angular white horse in the foreground, this painting shows a lady lying on the horse's back, as if in a circus-balancing act. The horse and the lady are about the same size, but the horse stands out as he does not have her faded coloration. Perhaps the horse represents the natural world while the circus-performing lady, the contrived world derived by the human imagination.

Painted in 1931, his second "Equestrienne" shows a lovely bluish-white horse with a blue mane, two pink flowers in his mouth, and a delicate saddle of flimsy white and blue cloth on his back, on top of which sits a well-dressed romantic couple. The horse, with a violin under his bowed head, is truly magical. In this picture with its fairytale ambience, the horse is utterly breathtaking.

Painted in 1942, "Scene Design for the Finale of the Ballet Aleko" portrays a white horse with spoked wheels at the base of his hind legs, hurling across the midnight sky. With its wavy mane flowing, the grand white horse recalls the ancient Greek mythological horses drawing gods' chariots through the night skies. A symbol of transcendence, this horse looks like an angel while simultaneously looking grotesque, For the horse and the wheels have become one, as the horse and its function for humankind converge into a single being in the mind's eye.

# Horse Sculptures

A striped terracotta horse with rider from the sixth century B.C.E. in Boeotia near Athens is among the many ancient equestrian sculptures likely created for religious or funerary purposes that reveal the importance of the horse in that society.[8] Sculptures of riders in chariots and carts pulled by horses, mounting and dismounting horses, horse racing, hunting on horseback, participating in farming, pageantry, and military action on horses have been the subject of equestrian sculptures since antiquity. The prized horse sculptures are cherished and preserved along with the mythologies from across the lands.

# Raymond Duchamp-Villon's "Horse"

"The power of the machine imposes itself upon us and we can scarcely conceive living bodies without it," writes the French artist Raymond Duchamp-Villon to a friend in 1913 while making sketches in preparation for his sculpture "Horse" which will have pistons and shafts for body parts.[9] Born in 1876, the artist Raymond Duchamp-Villon dies in 1918 without seeing the completion of his bronze sculpture "Horse" carried out by his brothers Jacques Villon and Marcel Duchamp in 1931.

Throughout his life, Raymond Duchamp-Villon is an expert horseman and a doctor in the cavalry, with both areas of expertise coming into play in his sculpture design. While his design is abstract, his sculpture totally captures and conveys the energy, power, and movement of a leaping horse.

The "Horse" sculpture has a presence that inspires its viewers to stop and think. As a symbol of power, beauty, life, death, time, freedom, and transcendence, the horse now shows up in art galleries and hence our dreams with machine body parts. The majestic animal, in whose company humans have enjoyed the rhythms of the natural world, has been morphed into images of the machines that contain us on the congested highways of our lives. The soothing neighs are now whirs. Our equestrian friends who take us to the castles in the skies of our imaginations are now machines.

# Shared History

Human and horse history has always been shared. Filled with lovely heartwarming adventures; glorious, terrifying, and thrilling escapades; and inspiring triumphs of survival, overcoming odds at great risk, and pushing against the limits of our strength and endurance, the history humans and horses share is as rich and varied as it is emotionally moving and spiritually uplifting. From exploring the horses' roles and characteristics in the mythologies and folk tales of many cultures throughout the ages as conveyed in stories once oral that have moved into many avenues of expression, from available art forms to evolving media, we can appreciate the depth of the history and bond that humans and horses share.

## Notes

1 Jonathan Swift, *Gulliver's Travels*. Ed. Tom Thomas (CA: Black Oyster, 2012), 183. Further references to this work appear parenthetically in this work.

2 Sylvia Plath, *Ariel* (NY: Harper & Row, 1965), 26. Further references to this work appear parenthetically in this work.

3 Christopher Brown, *Images of the Golden Past: Dutch Genre Painting of the 17th Century* (NY: Abbeville, 1984), 48. Further references to this work appear parenthetically in this work.

4 Francis Frascina, Nigel Blake, Briony Fer, Tamar Garb, and Charles Harrison, *Modernity and Modernism: French Painting in the Nineteenth Century* (New Haven and London: Yale UP, 1993), 233. Further references to this work appear parenthetically in this work.

5 William Morris and Robert Steele, *The Defence Of Guinevere and Other Poems* (London: Alexander Moring Ltd., De La More, 1904; Whitefish, MT: Kessinger Publishing's Legacy Reprint, 1974), xix. Further references to this work appear parenthetically in this work.

6 Sir Thomas Malory, *The Morte Darthur, An Abridgement with an Introduction*, eds. Charles Richard Sanders and Charles E. Ward (New York: Appleton-Century-Crofts, 1968). Further references to this work appear parenthetically in this work.

7 Maurice Raynal, *Modern Painting*, trans. Stuart Gilbert (Switzerland: Albert Skira, 1956), 162. Print.

8 Catherine Johns, *Horses: History, Math, Art* (Cambridge, MA: Harvard UP, 2006), 42. Further references to this work appear parenthetically in this work.

9 *Art Institute of Chicago: Raymond Duchamp-Villon, Horse* (Chicago: Studio Blue), Web. 18 Feb. 2016.

# CHAPTER 9

# Contemporary Horse Tales

## Horses in Action

Popular films reflect issues with which people wrestle and dreams for which they yearn. As such, filmmakers, or mythmakers, never cease to bring horse tales to life and, whether viewing films larger than life in theaters or in diminutive sizes on TV screens and handheld devices, worldwide audiences never cease to be drawn to the dreams these tales evoke.

Such notable horses in TV and film as the mighty steed Silver in *The Lone Ranger* (1933), *Black Beauty* (1946 film), Trigger in *Roy Rogers* (1950s), *Fury* (1950s-60s), Flicka in *My Friend Flicka* (1943 film and 1950s TV series), *Mister Ed* (1960s TV series), *The Horse Whisperer* (1998), *Horse Crazy* (2001), *The Saddle Club* (2001 TV series), *The Young Black Stallion* (2003), *Heartland* (2007 TV Series), and more, fed and still feed many of our fantasies and love of horses. They are the archetypes of loyalty, friendship, endurance, tolerance, bravery, beauty, and so much more. Each speaks or has spoken to our inner quests to be our best selves.

Watching these magnificent horses in action on our portable handheld devices in convenient locations, on our TV screens in our own living rooms, or as grand cinematic articulations of their stories as they heal after life-threatening injuries and win races against all odds, lifts the human spirit with a vitality that stirs and awakens our imaginations. Their abundant portrayals in films and other media reimagine horses again and again as the powerful, beautiful, and inspiring animals they are, enchanting audiences who love horses and see in the horses' strengths their own. This chapter offers a few examples and sheds light on how contemporary myth- or filmmakers reimagine horse tales reflecting the yearnings and inspirations of individuals and cultures. Finally, it speaks of humans' enduring love of swift powerful horses as expressed in myths and dreams that come to life on the silver screen.

## Equus

When the 1960's era—of fighting for civil rights, women's rights, and peace; of questioning social structures, powers of authority, and life's meaning; of counter-culture music and dancing in the streets; of redefining what we believe, wear, eat, and smoke—comes to a close, the stage-play *Equus* emerges, inviting audiences now settled into routines and humdrum lifestyles to question how deeply the outer realities they have pieced together actually satisfy the needs of their inner selves. Stunning horse-costumed characters populate the stage in the 1973 play Peter Shaffer writes awakening lust and longings within viewers who have sold their dreams for comfortable condos.

The central character, a disturbed seventeen-year-old boy named Alan Strang, blinds six horses. He is fascinated with horses, sexually attracted to horses, and has a desire to free horses of the bits they have in their mouths. For the boy, the horse is God. While the psychiatrist, Martin Dysart, attempts to "cure" him of his obsessions, the boy exhibits an intensity that casts light on the emptiness within the psychiatrist's heart which is mirrored in his dull relationships and life.

With a psychiatrist being portrayed trying to cure a young man of his pathological-religious fascination with horses that grows out of his mother's biblical tales, his grandfather's affection for horses and horse riding, and movies he watches, audiences are called to face their own inner drives. Following dramatic events that ensue leading the psychiatrist and the audience to question their passions and religious convictions, large numbers of theater goers depart entertained and awed by the power of the play—and the power of the horse.

In 1977, a movie version[1] is released in which the young Alan Strang (Peter Firth) and the psychiatrist (Richard Burton) hold nothing back. The boy's obsessions challenge the psychiatrist's view of his own limited reality in ways that move audiences to think. The horse is a vehicle, a powerful image; the horrors and complexities of the human mind, as dramatized, push audiences to wake up, look inside, and reassess what is most important to them.

## Seabiscuit

When the Great Depression hits the nation in the 1930s, people need something to believe in—and what better than a racehorse? Seabiscuit's exhilarating story is one of self-discovery and triumph. The 2003 movie based on Laura Hillenbrand's novel *Seabiscuit: An American Legend* (2001)[2] captures the spirit of hope that surrounds the horse as it wins races against all odds, giving audiences a renewed optimism and belief that they, much like the horse, can overcome their challenges and succeed.

For some, this story reflects our own personal journeys of recovery and survival: enabling us to feel we are not alone, giving us hope that we, too, can triumph. I had read about how the novel's author Laura Hillenbrand was struggling with the debilitating chronic fatigue syndrome while bringing Seabiscuit's story into the world, and I waited with baited breath for the movie's release. Not only is this story a journey of healing for the film's main characters (the horse, car dealer, cowboy, and horse jockey), but also for the book's author and many of its readers and viewers, such as myself. While chomping at the bit for the movie's release, I was undergoing treatment for the chronic disease Hepatitis C and receiving strength from knowing the author and her characters could push through to the other side. At its core, this is an inspiring tale of healing in mythic proportion. As stated in the movie's memorable dialog:

> Charles Howard (the car dealer) speaking to Red Pollard (the jockey): "You could be crippled for the rest of your life."
>
> Red Pollard: "I was crippled for the rest of my life. I got better. [Seabiscuit] made me better. Hell, you made me better."[3]

Connecting with the personal triumphs of the author Hillenbrand, the horse, and the movies well-defined and portrayed characters makes many of us in the audience better.

The story is of Seabiscuit's journey as he evolves from an underachieving horse to a legend on the racetrack. His owner, Charles Howard (Jeff Bridges) is a car dealer who goes from rags to riches, meets with tragedy, and invests in a dream of winning. He hires an old down-and-out cowboy, Tom Smith (Chris Cooper), to train Seabiscuit, and a half-blind jockey, Red Pollard (Tobey Maguire), to ride him. The story about broken men taking a chance on a little horse inspires a nation devastated by the depression and engenders the hope of a future for people just trying to hang on and get better. As Tom Smith, the horse trainer in the movie, concludes: "You know, you don't throw a whole life away just because he's banged up a little," a message the movie clearly articulates.

## Secretariat

When life is growing grim, why not bet it on a horse? This horse tale, presented on the silver screen (2010), captures the heartbeat and hoof beat of the horse that wins the Triple Crown in 1973, a feat of great horse racing magnitude being the first such win in twenty-five years. Based on William Nack's novel *Secretariat: The Making of a Champion* (2002), this is another uplifting horse tale audiences can believe in. As the horse's owner and film's protagonist Penny Chenery (Diane Lane), who learns to believe in herself and act on her convictions, declares: "This is not about going back. This is about life being ahead of you and you run at it! Because you never know how far you can run unless you run."[4]

Journeys of the remarkable horse Secretariat and his owner Penny Chenery who seems willing to sacrifice everything for her dreams that include making him a champion, come to life in vivid splendor. This is the story of a horse that shows promise and a woman willing to bet her life on his potential and her instincts, a feel-good tale of a horse with talent and a woman who believes in him. Yet, it is more.

Anyone who loses a parent or is close to an ill or dying parent and must keep the business of life going amidst the turmoil of dysfunctional family relationships, can relate to the struggles depicted and overcome in this story. When her mother dies and her ill Virginia farm-owner father (Scott Glen) is unable to carry on, Penny Chenery (Diane Lane), part of a family that wants to sell the farm, refuses to sell. She flips a coin and wins a mare that gives birth to Secretariat, an untested horse for which she turns down a seven-million dollar offer. Leaving her husband Jack Tweedy (Dylan Walsh) and children behind in Colorado, she heads to Virginia to run the farm against her family's wishes.

With the convincing Diane Lane playing the compelling Penny Chenery, a woman with the guts to trust her own judgement and act on her own convictions as she bets on a farm and a racehorse, the movie charms audiences of all ages, bringing to life the mythic tale of a woman's success—with the help of her hired horse trainer Lucien Laurin (John Malkovich)—in a male-dominated business, ultimately breeding and raising the first Triple Crown winner in twenty-five years. This is a horse tale that wins audiences' hearts, as they vicariously feel the pains and exhilaration of Penny Chenery's and Secretariat's efforts to move forward and secure victory.

## War Horse

*War Horse*, a stage-production hit originating at London's National Theater (2007) and a subsequent cinematic sensation (2011) based on Michael Morpurgo's children's novel by the same name (1982),[5] continues to thrill audiences worldwide. Set in WWI, the heartwarming love story centers around a horse named Joey and a boy named Albert who trains and tames him on a family farm in England, who then are parted and strive to reconnect.

Audiences flock to the London stage to see life-sized horse puppets built primarily of pliable bamboo come to life through the skill of puppeteers. A gripping tale set in the early twentieth century recounts the story of a farm boy who, after training his horse to pull a plough and in the process befriending and growing to love his horse, is devastated with the news that his drunken father has sold the horse for cash to a young officer in the cavalry at the outbreak of World War I. The heartbreaking events result in the boy's enlisting in the Army to find his horse and bring him home.

Connecting with audiences' deep-seated memories of their beloved childhood pets, this horse tale stirs emotions, inspiring audiences to press through obstacles to preserve their relationships and achieve their goals and dreams. The horse tale's sentiments are captured in the main character Albert Narracott's words as he comforts his horse Joey: "We'll be alright Joey. We're the lucky ones, you and me. Lucky since the day I met you."

Steven Spielberg is so moved by the magnificent performance that he makes a movie[6] version, bringing the story to a wider audience. In the film version, real horses replace the puppetry thereby creating the opportunity to see magnificent horses bigger than life in action on the silver screen. The message of the novel that comes to life on stage and in sensational cinematic artistry is of the horrors of war in which multitudes of humans and animals suffer and die. The tremendous loss of life, particularly the vast numbers of horses' lives, is the reality of the cost of war that this horse tale's viewers cannot escape.

## Timeless Horse Tales

The inherent interest in timeless horse tales continues. As a result, horses are reimagined over and over in vivid grandeur, grazing and galloping in varying landscapes, with their journeys of triumph and friendship mirroring the faces of our enduring needs during changing times. With their speed and flair, they reconnect us with the dust of an earlier age as our hearts and cultures move from fascination with horses to horse races.

## California Chrome and American Pharoah

The multi-million-dollar horse race industry attracts exuberant crowds who are willing to bet their dreams (and bank accounts) on a horse. One of the horses that grips the hearts of so many is California Chrome. This horse and his owners offer a rags-to-riches tale that inspires millions of people to believe in the impossible dream once again. An American thoroughbred racehorse who wins the 2014 Kentucky Derby and the Preakness Stakes, then goes on to Belmont Park to try for the Triple Crown, generates tremendous excitement.

While fans let out roars in support of California Chrome, the horse attempts but fails to win the Triple Crown. A year later with fans once again cheering and waving, American Pharoah becomes the first horse since 1978 to sweep the Triple Crown. With some in the crowd able to remember watching Secretariat win the Belmont by thirty-one lengths, this win still dazzles. American Pharoah wins hearts and big bucks with his impressive athletic build, natural and well-trained talent, and stunning high-speed performance. The crowds never cease to show up to bet on their dreams, with the horse being the mythological symbol of transport and transcendence.

As films, novels, and horse race attractions reveal, horses imagined in tales or experienced on farms or racetracks have the capacity to move human imaginations. Mythic horses like Seabiscuit, Secretariat, the War Horse named Joey, California Chrome, and American Pharoah reflect the journeys of those of us who imagine ourselves finding the courage to take chances, push forward, and express our inner natures no matter the costs, thereby making our dreams come alive. Maybe betting on a racehorse is an opportunity to validate one's own hunches—or is a metaphor for taking a chance on living (as opposed to going through) life.

## Horse Tales on YouTubes

The inherent interest in timeless horse tales continues as evidenced by the countless number of YouTubes being posted daily by people of all ages and locations who delight in sharing fanciful yet heartfelt stories of how humans and horses depend on each other for survival. Many portray horse trainers' and others' enchantment with horses, as well as their concerns and recommended best practices in caring for horses. Easily accessible, horse imagery continues to live on in our imaginations and dreams as expressed and conveyed in a plethora of YouTubes. A couple of examples follow.

*The Path of the Horse*

A woman's childhood passion for horses and subsequent career as a horse trainer takes a turn. She decides to embark on a quest to meet with those who might impart wisdom to her about how to learn from and be with horses in more authentic ways. Ultimately, she learns that to be in authentic relationships with horses and other beings begins with letting go and becoming authentic from within. Exquisitely portrayed is an unfolding of how to still her mind, achieve a balance between meditation and activity, appreciate horses' desires, feelings, and needs, and be in fulfilling relationships with horses not by riding them but by being with them. From this YouTube comes the lovely message that we may have more to learn from horses than the other way around.[7]

*Most Beautiful Horse Film Ever*

No words. Serene instrumental music serenades as horses in the open air gracefully touch their hoofs to the sand creating sand clouds all around the horses. Running together, herds of black, brown, and white horses dash through grassy fields and sandy plains. Walking, leaping, and galloping in slow motion, horses gracefully move as in a dance. Close-ups of horse heads, then of two horses romping, sparing, and joining together as if kissing, are among the images all strung together like pearls to create this most enchanting YouTube.[8] Herds of horses trotting along seem to keep time with the mystical music. Absolutely delicious, awe-inspiring, and mood elevating, this YouTube brings each horse to life like a lover seen through the eyes of his or her partner.

# Musical Horse Tales

Whether singing songs aloud alone or with friends, listening to music live in concert halls or from electronic and digital devices in the comfort of our cars and living rooms, or tuning into streaming services using earbuds while riding, swimming, running, gardening, cooking, or cleaning, the rhythmic sounds and beats fill our heads with hoof prints of galloping horses.

"Wild horses couldn't drag me away" are among the passionate lyrics touching hearts across the decades as a variety of artists are moved to record The Rolling Stones' song "Wild Horses" in their own ways. From The Rolling Stones' recording in 1971 to Susan Boyle's in 2009 and others, comes the promise of wild horses being unable to drag the vocalist away from his or her devotion. Convincing and reassuring, the thought that no amount or strength of horses or horsepower could lead the person away or avert their commitment is overwhelmingly persuasive and speaks volumes.

"A Horse with No Name" by the folk/rock group America is an American hit that topped the charts in several countries, reaching gold in 1972. The meaning of the horse in this song changes with each listener but could easily represent a getaway vehicle or the horses in many myths on which riders transcend their realities and soar to the castles of their imaginations in the stars or fly like the wind between worlds mortal and divine. Having no name makes the horse marvelously mysterious and free of labels and entrapments.

English singer, songwriter, and composer Elton John delivered "Live Like Horses" in 1997, sending the message that the ability to regain our senses belongs to those who break out of their stalls and live like horses, with horses being a metaphor for the freedom of living in the moment without personal baggage. American singer and songwriter Taylor Swift released the hit song "White Horse" in 2008 connecting childhood fantasies of prince charming on a white horse coming to sweep her and, by association, us off our feet and save us, with the disappointment of a failed love relationship and the need to move on and take care of ourselves. With her song, she broadcasts the message that life is not a fairytale. Since the white horse has notoriously been the steed of heroes and saints in many fairytales and myths, a trend that is widely challenged and changing, her lyrics are easily understood and register with a wide audience.

From country to contemporary music, horse songs always fill the sound waves. Some speak of the love and friendship humans and horses share and the thrill of riding together, while others use the horse as an example of how to live. The horse tales continue with every beat.

# Horse Tales:  Moving Forward

With the many available media options, people may gain instant worldwide access around the clock to the myriad ways in which cultures choose to portray horses, with adults and children, or god, goddesses, and assorted mythological characters riding them through colorful canyons and magical forests, across turbulent seas, and above luminescent skies beyond the moon and back again, or engaging and befriending them, listening to them, and caring for their needs as they cozy up to us and attend to ours. The fact that the majestic animals continue to inspire us, and that horse myths keep moving into the latest media, reveals that the love between humans and horses is deep, ever-present, and enriches our lives.

The ancients and people of today experience and understand myths according to their cultural canons. Myths answer a need, an inner pulsing, an aspiration, or a yearning, on both a personal and collective level. Therefore, the extensive presence of horse tales that originate in the oral storytelling tradition of early civilizations, then move into print, paintings, stage productions, cinema, television, and songs, and are now available on the Internet in YouTubes, podcasts, streaming videos, and e-books, demonstrates how deeply equine images permeate our personal psyches and remain living burning realities within the collective psyche—and moves horse myths forward.

## Notes


1 *Equus*, Perf. Richard Burton, Peter Firth; Dir. Sidney Lumet (Prod. MGM. 1977), DVD.

2 Laura Hillenbrand, *Seabiscuit, An American Legend* (NY: Ballentine, 2001). Further references to this work appear parenthetically in this work.

3 *Seabiscuit*, Perf. Tobey Maguire, Jeff Bridges, Chris Cooper; Dir. Gary Ross; Filmmaker Steven Soderbergh (Prod. Universal and DreamWorks, 2003), DVD.

4 *Secretariat.* Dir. Randall Wallace; Perf. Diane Lane, John Malkovich (Prod. Walt Disney Pictures, 2010), DVD.

5 Michael Morpurgo, *War Horse* (London: Egmont, 1982). Further references to this work appear parenthetically in this work.

6 *War Horse*, Perf. Emily Watson, David Thewlis; Dir. Steven Spielberg (Prod. Touchstone Pictures, 2012), DVD.

7 *The Path of the Horse - Full Length Documentary* (Our Horses, 2012), YouTube.

8 *Most Beautiful Horse Film Ever*, ed. AmRambo. Composer, James Lambrecht (AmRambo, 2012.), YouTube.

# CHAPTER 10

# Horsepower vs Horse Survival

## Horse Tales: Moving Forward

Horse tales' migration into contemporary media is evidence that our journey together, human and horse, speaks to people today. Humans now living in urban hives may only know about horses through their experiences of watching them perform in product campaigns or stories on their computer screens and convenient handheld devices. Product manufacturers and marketers bank on their current and potential customers' enduring love of horses.

For decades car manufacturers have named their cars after horses making their customers' love of horses and horse-riding conscious, making it possible for us all to buy our dream of hopping on a horse and riding off into the sunset by buying our dream cars. Car companies know that connecting their products with our passion for horses will bring them the big bucks, and many car companies hop on board.

The Ford Motor Company unleashes the "Ford Mustang" automotive vehicle in the 1960s. The company employs the name that directly links their cars with Mustang horses, which are best known for their stamina and speed and often for being full-bodied and hot-blooded, though the horses' characteristics are wide-ranging. The term *Mustang* is from the Spanish word *mestena*, meaning wild or stray. These horses are the offspring of the horses that roamed around America ten-thousand years ago, then vanished, and re-emerged with the Spanish conquistadors in the sixteenth century, transforming Native American lives.

The Ford Motor Company then puts the "Ford Bronco" on the scene in the mid-1960s through the mid-1990s. The term is from the Spanish word *bronco*, meaning rough and references horses across North America that are wild and untrained, and habitually buck. Giving cars this name associates the vehicles with the idea of a rough and wild ride, appealing to the tough and tough-minded folks who want to buy the power-cars for charging forth on any terrain.

In the 1960s, Mitsubishi brings to market a sub-compact car called the "Mitsubishi Colt" naming it after the horse that is male and young, usually below the age of four years. Chrysler, the company's partner, then introduces the "Dodge Colt" and "Plymouth Colt" in the 1970s and beyond into 1994. Using the name "Colt" not only associates these cars with their potential buyers' deep-seated love of horses, but with the image of an attractive person who has a magnanimous personality and gets along well with everyone. With the purchase of the automobile, customers can buy not only the car, but the image.

Hyundai is not to be left in the dust. With the term *Equus* being the Latin word for "horse", the South Korean car manufacturer, Hyundai Motor Co. of Korea, introduces the "Hyundai Equus" into the United States market in 2003 with a new improved model coming out in 2009, and others following.

While some companies name their cars after horses, other companies might make their cars' connections to horses more subtle, by naming them after Greek gods and goddesses instead, as in the "Nissan Titan", "Buick Apollo", "Lincoln Zephyr", and "Honda Odyssey", or naming them after birds, epic events, or simply giving them acronyms or numbers. The cars' connection to horses is palpable and inescapable, nevertheless. Horses have historically enabled humans to travel farther and faster than they could otherwise; in effect, giving humans wings. Cars now offer humans this gift or capability.

Today, urbanites and suburbanites hop into and connect with their high-horsepower vehicles, then dart onto the freeways just as their forbears would mount and ride their beloved hoofed-friends into the sunset with dreams of dashing beyond the heavens on winged horses that likely have morphed into today's jets, rocketry, and drones. As images of mutual human and horse existences are thrust into cyberspace via YouTubes, podcasts, Facebook, video games, and other technologies, the hope is that our shared journeys will be meaningful to future generations—and preserved.

## The Human-Horse Story

With the prevalence of horse stories being expressed in so many art forms, horses are reimagined over and over as the majestic animals they are in their natural settings, and as symbols of strength, endurance, and transcendence in our mythology, folklore, and the literary and fine arts, offering humans images of companionship, transcendence, and hope throughout our changing times. Now, with their speed and beauty, they reconnect us with the dust of an earlier age as our hearts and cultures move from fascination with horses to horse races—and horsepower.

Today's urban and suburban dwellers do not live with and rely on horses' swiftness and power for transportation, strength for pulling carts, agility and adeptness for sport, and loyalty and friendship as did the home dwellers who lived near fields and prairies in earlier societies as well as those today who live in rural cultures. Yet, the magnificent steeds—even if only known to contemporary city dwellers through their exposure to equine images in the media and other art forms—remain strong in our psyches today. Now, impressed with their speed and style, many people mount and befriend their cars with the same passion their forebears honored and worked their horses. While many of us today enjoy riding and caring for our beloved horses, the myth has morphed from horse heroes to horsepower.

Today we urbanites and suburbanites love our urban horses, or high-horsepower cars designed to perform. We feed them high-priced gas, or electric vehicle charges, and show off their muscular and elegant body-styling as they outperform speed limits. While public transportation and ridesharing can reduce the traffic on our crowded streets and freeways, participating requires abandoning our love of charging forth on horses, now high-horsepower vehicles. Making such a shift would propel our love of horses and horseback riding toward that of sustaining horses on earth and with them, other species including ourselves.

In today's world of limited natural resources and the impact of climate change from human activity, perhaps it is time to make our age-old fascination with horses conscious. Instead of cherishing the freedom to jump on our urban horses or high-horsepower vehicles and ride, we might instead embrace the beauty of saving the horse and ourselves. Making deeply-rooted life changes from riding to ridesharing, from impulsively hopping into cars and driving places instead to selectively organizing fewer outings, from valuing the freedom to ride forth instead to valuing the freedom to remain centered within ourselves and our living spaces, from going out instead to going within and seeing ourselves for who we really are: these are small steps for consideration that can make a big difference toward a sustainable future.

Myths provide constructs that make order out of chaos. Today, if we can see the wonderment in horses and the natural world, and allow it to awaken our imaginations, then perhaps we can embrace myths about developing lifestyles that are in accord with nature—ones that champion the protection of horses, humans, and the environment.

In this historic hour, perhaps it is time to allow tales of horses to empower and inspire us to take life by the reins or, better yet, to let go and listen to the horses. Thank you.

# Bibliography

Adams, Michael Vannoy. *The Mythological Unconscious*. London: H. Karnac, 2001. Print.

Alexander, Skye. *Unicorns, the Myths, Legends, and Lore*. Avon, MA: Adams Media, 2015. Print.

Andrews, Tamra. *Dictionary of Nature Myths*. Oxford: Oxford UP, 1998. Print.

*Art Institute of Chicago: Raymond Duchamp-Villon, Horse*. Chicago, IL: Studio Blue. Web. 18 Feb 2016.

Bond, D. Stephenson. *Living Myth: Personal Meaning as a Way of Life*. Boston, MA: Shambhala, 1993. Print.

Brown, Christopher. *Images of the Golden Past: Dutch Genre Painting of the 17th Century*. NY: Abbeville, 1984. Print.

Campbell, Joseph. *The Flight of the Wild Gander: Explorations in the Mythological Dimension (Selected Essays 1944-1968)*. Novato, CA: New World Library, 2002. Print.

---. *The Masks of God: Creative Mythology*. NY: Penguin Books, 1976. Print.

---. *The Power of Myth with Bill Moyers*. Ed. Betty Sue Flowers. NY: Broadway, 2001. Print.

Chang, Isabelle C. *Chinese Fairy Tales*. NY: Shocken, 1965. Print.

Chevalier, Jean and Alain Gheerbrant. *The Penguin Dictionary of Symbols*. Trans. John Buchanan-Brown. NY: Penguin, 1996. Print.

Cohen, Barbara. "White Horse Temple," *Destinations: Vietnam / Hanoi*. Things Asian, 1995. Web. Feb. 17, 2016.

Coogan, Michael D., ed. *The New Oxford Annotated Bible, Third Edition with the Apocryphal/ Deuterocanonical Books: New Revised Standard Version*. Oxford UP, 2001. Print.

Cooper, J. C. *An Illustrated Encyclopaedia of Traditional Symbols.* NY: Thames and Hudson, 1979. Print.

Crossley-Holland, Kevin. *The Norse Myths.* NY: Pantheon, 1980. Print.

Davis, F. Hadland. *Myths and Legends of Japan.* NY: Dover, 1992. Print.

Deloria, Jr., Vine and Daniel R. Wildcat. *Power and Place: Indian Education in America.* Golden, CO: Fulcrum Resources, 2001. Print.

Edwards, Elwyn Hartley. *The Encyclopedia of the Horse: The Definitive Guide to the Horse: the Major Breeds of the World, Their History & Modern Use.* London, New York, Stuttgart, Moscow: Dorling Kindersley Book, 1994. Print.

*Equus.* Perf. Richard Burton, Peter Firth. Dir. Sidney Lumet. Prod. MGM. 1977. DVD.

Erdoes, Richard and Alfonso Ortiz, eds. *American Indian Myths and Legends.* NY: Pantheon, 1984. Print.

Frascina, Francis, Nigel Blake, Briony Fer, Tamar Garb, and Charles Harrison. *Modernity and Modernism: French Painting in the Nineteenth Century.* New Haven and London: Yale UP, 1993. Print.

Fuller, C. J. *The Camphor Flame: Popular Hinduism and Society in India.* Princeton UP, 1992. Print.

Getty, Alice. *The Gods of Northern Buddhism: Their History and Iconography.* NY: Dover, 1988. Print.

Goble, Paul. *The Girl Who Loved Wild Horses.* NY: Aladdin, 1978. Print.

Graves, Robert. *The Greek Myths, Complete Edition.* London: Penguin Books, 1955. Print.

Green, Miranda. *Animals in Celtic Life and Myth.* London and NY: Routledge, 1992. Print.

---. *Dictionary of Celtic Myth and Legend.* London: Thames and Hudson, 1992. Print.

Grimal, Pierre. *The Penguin Dictionary of Classical Mythology.* Trans. A.R. Maxwell-Hyslop. Oxford, England: Blackwell, 1991. Print.

Hausman, Gerald and Loretta. *The Mythology of Horses: Horse Legend and Lore Throughout the Ages.* NY: Three Rivers, 2003. Print.

Hillenbrand, Laura. *Seabiscuit, An American Legend.* NY: Ballentine, 2001. Print.

*The Holy Scriptures. Revised in Accordance with Jewish Tradition and Modern Biblical Scholarship.* NY: Hebrew Publishing Co., 1939. Print.

Howey, M. Olden. *The Horse in Magic and Myth.* Mineola, NY: Dover, 2002. Print.

Hunt, August. *The Terrible One's Horse: Revealing the Secrets of Norse Myth.* Stag Spirit Books, 2012. Print.

Jackson, Sophie. *The Horse in Myth and Legend.* Gloucestershire: Tempus, 2006. Print.

Johns, Catherine. *Horses: History, Math, Art.* Cambridge, MA: Harvard UP, 2006. Print.

Jung, Carl G. *Dreams.* Trans. R.F.C. Hull. Bollingen Series XX. Princeton: Princeton UP, 1974. Print.

---. *Symbols of Transformation: An Analysis of a Prelude to a Case of Schizophrenia.* Bollingen Series XX. NY: Pantheon, 1956. Print.

Leeming, David A. *The Handy Mythology Answer Book.* MI: Visible Ink, 2015. Print.

Leighton, Taigen Dan. *Faces of Compassion: Classic Bodhisattva Archetypes and Their Modern Expression.* Boston, MA: Wisdom Publications, 2003. Print.

Macgregor-Morris, Pamela, ed. *The Book of the Horse.* NY: Exeter, 1979. Print.

Malory, Sir Thomas. *The Morte Darthur, An Abridgement with an Introduction.* Eds. Charles Richard Sanders and Charles E. Ward. NY: Appleton-Century-Crofts, 1968. Print.

Mathews, Thomas F. *The Clash of Gods: A Reinterpretation of Early Christian Art, Revised and Expanded Edition.* Princeton and Oxford: Princeton UP, 1993. Print.

McNeese, Tim, Ed. *Myths of Native America.* NY: Four Walls Eight Windows, 1999. Print.

Morpurgo, Michael. *War Horse.* London: Egmont, 1982. Print.

Morris, William and Robert Steele. *The Defence Of Guinevere and Other Poems*. (London: Alexander Moring Ltd., De La More, 1904.) Whitefish, MT: Kessinger Publishing's Legacy Reprint, 1974. Print.

*Most Beautiful Horse Film Ever*. Ed. AmRambo. Composer, James Lambrecht. AmRambo, 2012. YouTube. Feb. 18 2016.

Nabokov, Peter, Ed. *Native American Testimony: A Chronicle of Eastern-White Relations from Prophecy to the Present, 1492-2000 (rev Edition)*. NY: Penguin, 1999. Print.

NicMhacha, Sharynne MacLeod. *Queen of the Night: Rediscovering the Celtic Moon Goddess*. Boston, MA: Weiser, 2005. Print.

*The Path of the Horse - Full Length Documentary*. OurHorses, 2012. YouTube. 9 Dec. 2015.

Perrin, Pat, ed. *Horses in Myths, Legends, Folktales, and Other Ancient Stories*. Lexington, KY: Madeira, 2014. Print.

Plath, Sylvia. *Ariel*. NY: Harper & Row, 1965. Print.

Raynal, Maurice. *Modern Painting*. Trans. Stuart Gilbert. Switzerland: Albert Skira, 1956. Print.

Rolleston, T. W. *Celtic Myths and Legends*. NY: Dover, 1990. Print.

Rowling, J.K. "Chapter 22, Hippogriff (Year 3)," *The Serpent's Heart, Draco Malfoy Reader X*. Harry Potter and Pottermore, Pottermore Limited. Warner Bros. Entertainment. N.d. Web. 18 January 2016

*Seabiscuit*. Perf. Tobey Maguire, Jeff Bridges, Chris Cooper. Dir. Gary Ross. Filmmaker. Steven Soderbergh. Prod. Universal and Dreamworks, 2003. DVD.

*Secretariat*. Dir. Randall Wallace. Perf. Diane Lane, John Malkovich. Prod. Walt Disney Pictures, 2010. DVD.

Shakespeare, William. *The Life of Henry V*. Ed. John Russell Brown. NY and Ontario: Signet Classic, New American Library, 1965. Print.

Sherman, Josepha. *Magic Hoofbeats: Horse Tales from Many Lands*. Cambridge, MA: Barefoot, 2004. Print.

Silko, Leslie Marmon. *Storyteller*. NY: Arcade, 1981. Print.

Singer, Isaac Bashevis and Margot Zemach. *Naftali the Storyteller and*

*His Horse, Sus, and Other Stories.* NY: Farrar, Straus and Giroux, 1976. Print.

Snyder, Gary. *A Place in Space: Ethics, Aesthetics, and Watersheds.* NY: Counterpoint, 1995. Print.

Summers, Gilbert. *Walkers Traditions of Scotland.* Cambridge: Martin Books, 1991. Print.

Swift, Jonathan. *Gulliver's Travels.* Ed. Tom Thomas. CA: Black Oyster, 2012. Print.

*War Horse.* Perf. Emily Watson, David Thewlis. Dir. Steven Spielberg. Prod. Touchstone Pictures, 2012. DVD.

Zimmer, Heinrich. *Myths and Symbols in Indian Art and Civilization.* Ed. Joseph Campbell. Bollingen Series VI. Princeton: Princeton UP, 1972. Print.

# Acknowledgements

I heard a neigh. Oh, such a brisk and melodious
neigh it was. My very heart leapt with the sound.

–Nathaniel Hawthorne

To the horses romping in the fields nearby, thank you for bringing me back to the natural world. Your beauty ever-majestic and frolicking ever-engaging, give this work meaning. In humility, I thank you.

To the storytellers, mythologists, artists, poets, authors, playwrights, filmmakers, composers, musicians, dancers, and others across time and place, who bring us transcendental blue horses, winged horses, and prisms and glasses through which to see horses and ourselves from many angles as we befriend horses and ride them to the sandcastles of our dreams, thank you for expanding our vision, sensibilities, and soulful journeys.

With appreciation, I would like to acknowledge and extend my thanks to the following for their contributions:

- To those whose writings about horses, horse tales, and equine images have informed this work;

- To Joseph Campbell, James Hillman, and professors and friends at Pacifica Graduate Institute, for demonstrating integrity and soulfulness in their work and lives in ways that have influenced my thinking and this work;

- To Catherine Ann Jones, author of *The Way of Story* and *Heal Your Self with Writing*, for reading my manuscript midstream and offering helpful comments;

- To Dr. Susan Paidhrin, whose great kindness in both reading my manuscript and providing reflections have added depth to my journey;

- To Marcie Medof, for graciously introducing me to the inspiring tale in Paul Goble's book, *The Girl Who Loved Wild Horses.*

Finally, I would like to acknowledge Pegasus and all the wondrous mythological horses for inspiring many of us to reach for the stars.

**Permissions Acknowledgements**

Grateful acknowledgement is extended to the following publishers for kindly granting their permission to paraphrase or reprint excerpts from previously published material:

- 'Lone Boy and the Old Dun Horse' and 'The Caspian Horse/ The Colt Qeytas' reproduced from MAGIC HOOFBEATS by kind permission of Barefoot Books, Inc. Text copyright ©Josepha Sherman. Illustrations copyright © Linda Wingerter. All rights reserved.

- THE COLLECTED POEMS OF SYLVIA PLATH, EDITED by TED HUGHES. Copyright (c) 1960, 1965, 1971, 1981 by the Estate of Sylvia Plath. Editorial material copyright (c) 1981 by Ted Hughes. Courtesy of HarperCollins Publishers.

- COLLECTED POEMS BY SYLVIA PLATH, Faber and Faber Ltd.

- THE MYTHOLOGY OF HORSES, HAUSMAN, Three Rivers Press.

# About the Author

**Janet Bubar Rich, Ph.D.**

With a love of mythology and storytelling, Dr. Janet Bubar Rich investigates timeless myths with a focus on the contemporary concerns of our world. Her books include:

- *Exploring Guinevere's Search for Authenticity* (Edwin Mellen Press, 2012), and

- *Hestia—Goddess of the Hearth* (Edwin Mellen Press, 2014).

A writer and editor based in Southern California, Janet holds a B.A. in English from UC Berkeley and a Ph.D. in Mythology / Depth Psychology from Pacifica Graduate Institute. When not writing, she can often be found sailing with her husband and dog in Marina del Rey.